the BINGE WATCHER'S guide

DOCTOR WHO:

A HISTORY OF DOCTOR WHO AND THE FIRST FEMALE DOCTOR

Mackenzie Flohr

For more information contact:
Riverdale Avenue Books
5676 Riverdale Avenue
Riverdale, NY 10471.

www.riverdaleavebooks.com
Design by www.formatting4U.com
Cover by Scott Carpenter

Digital ISBN: 9781626015234
Trade Paperback ISBN: 9781626015241
Hardcover ISBN: 9781626015258

First Edition, December 2019

There are fixed points throughout time where things must stay exactly the way they are.

This is not one of them, this is an opportunity. Whatever happens here will create its own timeline, its own reality, a temporal tipping point.

The future revolves around you, here, now, so do good!

-Chris Chibnall

This book is dedicated to all the fans who have made *Doctor Who* possible, for without you, there would be no show; therefore, no books.

Table of Contents

Introduction

Don't be scared. All of this is new to you, and new can be scary. Now we all want answers. Stick with me— you might get some.
- 13th Doctor

Doctor Who has an impeccable ability to change people's worlds. Whether they're fans of the show or involved in its production, it has touched so many people in so many ways. I was a young child when my dad first introduced me to The Doctor, back when Peter Davison was behind the iconic role. It was being broadcast on our local PBS station at the time, and my parents still owned one of those really old televisions that had six channels max. Honestly, I can't remember why I loved the fifth incarnation of The Doctor as much as I did, but perhaps it was simply because he was my *first* Doctor.

The thing that any long-time fan of the show will tell you is that you'll always remember your first. First impressions are important after all, which is why when a new actor steps into those shoes it's kind of a big deal.

When it was announced in 2017 that the next actor to take the reins of The Doctor's big blue police box (the TARDIS or Time and Relative Dimension in Space, for those in the know) would be revealed after the

Wimbledon Men's Final, I found myself eagerly waiting for the match to end. *The Sun*, a UK newspaper, had previously reported an alleged leak stating that British actor Kris Marshall was going to be the new *Doctor Who*, and that he had already started filming. Whether this was meant to be a misdirect or just false information however, lives were about to be changed.

On July 16, 2017, *Doctor Who* fans around the world were treated to a minute-long reveal trailer. This was something that had never been done before! Normally, a new Doctor would be introduced to the fandom through an interview, or simply a previously recorded hello from the actor. But this time was special. This time fans got to experience a scene exclusively with the new owner of the TARDIS.

If you're new to *Doctor Who* or didn't get the chance to experience it, picture this: You are transported to a scene in the middle of a forest. The sun is out, the birds are singing, and the camera pans to the back of our new Doctor. They're walking through the foliage in a long gray wool trench coat, in search of the TARDIS. The music is suspenseful, if not a little bit creepy, composed by Segun Akinola. As the camera closes in on The Doctor's dark brown boots, they step on a large stick snapping it in the process.

The Doctor stops.

You can hear the distinct whooshing sound of the TARDIS in the background as it begins to materialize. The camera switches now, focusing in on The Doctor's right hand. It's a young hand, perhaps nervous due to the nails being worn down. As the hand opens to take possession of the key to the TARDIS, another surprise. It appears to be feminine. Once more the angle changes, focusing on the face hidden beneath the cloak's dark hood.

And as The Doctor pulls back the cowl, a woman smiles back at the audience as her TARDIS materializes in front of her. The credits reveal the 13th Doctor to be none other than Jodie Whittaker.

So, why was that minute-long reveal trailer so significant? *Doctor Who* fans that day witnessed something that had never been done before in the show's 50 plus year history! The lead role of The Doctor, who had been up to this point only ever been portrayed by a man, was for the first time, going to be interpreted by a woman.

When Chris Chibnall, the new showrunner of *Doctor Who*, was interviewed about his decision to cast a female Doctor, he said: "I always knew I wanted the 13th Doctor to be a woman and we're thrilled to have secured our number one choice. Her audition for The Doctor simply blew us all away. Jodie is an in-demand, funny, inspiring, super-smart force of nature and will bring loads of wit, strength and warmth to the role. The 13th Doctor is on her way."

Christel Dee and Luke Spillane, from *The Doctor Who: Fan Show*, filmed their live reactions to the reveal of the new Doctor.

"For me as a girl, like, this is something I never thought would be possible… ever. I always, always, ruled it out," said Christel.

"*Doctor Who* is at its best when it actually makes big, bold changes. And this will be marked in its 50 plus years as one of the three or four changes they have made. The first, being the concept of regeneration. This is huge," said Luke.

When interviewed by BBC Worldwide, Charlotte Moore, Director of BBC Content, agreed: "Making history is what *Doctor Who* is all about and Chris Chibnall's bold new take on the next Time Lord is exactly that. The nation is going to fall in love with Jodie Whittaker—and have lots of fun, too!"

Even Peter Capaldi, who at the time was playing the 12th incarnation of *Doctor Who,* had wonderful things to say about Jodie Whittaker's casting: "Anyone who has seen Jodie Whittaker's work will know that she is a wonderful actress of great individuality and charm. She has above all the huge heart to play this most special part. She's going to be a fantastic Doctor."

* * *

In just one day, Jodie Whittaker's Doctor reveal had been viewed over 16 million times on BBC social media channels. Piers Wenger, Controller of BBC Drama, stated in a BBC press release: "To see the overwhelmingly positive response to the news that Jodie Whittaker will star as the 13th Doctor and know that the reveal has had over 16 million views online so far, is just phenomenal. It's exhilarating to see *Doctor Who* engaging with people on so many different levels and I cannot wait for the audience to see her in action on BBC One this Christmas."

To be honest, I wasn't 100% on board with a female Doctor at first. I was familiar with Jodie Whittaker through the series *Broadchurch*, which Chris Chibnall wrote and had won awards for, and her portrayal of Beth was extraordinary; it wasn't her personally that I had a problem with. The Doctor had always been portrayed by male actors, that's what I had grown up with. My problem was that I didn't want to accept change, which is so ironic because that's really what *Doctor Who* is all about—change.

After sleeping on it for 24 hours, I got to thinking about the idea of a female Doctor. *Why can't we have a Doctor that's female? Doctors can be female too, after all, and I absolutely adore Michelle Gomez's performance as Missy, an antagonist in the previous season.* I also love cosplaying as The Doctor, and realized having The Doctor be female, would make my cosplays more canon! That was when I truly started getting excited about Jodie Whittaker's casting.

This past May I had the opportunity to sign books at Motor City Comic Con, a convention in Novi, Michigan. I met some fantastic *Doctor Who* fans, and some of them admitted to me that Jodie was already their favorite Doctor. I was thrilled! I hadn't heard anyone say that yet. For a new doctor to already be that beloved further proved to me that the 13th Doctor was going to be in good hands.

Truthfully, I didn't need other fans to convince me. I only had to look at the ratings. The first episode of her series, for example, drew the biggest launch viewing figures in 10 years. According to overnight ratings, an average of 8.2 million tuned in to watch, with a peak of nine million and an audience share of 40.1%. As the ninth incarnation would say, that's fantastic!

* * *

Riverdale Avenue Books has set out to do something that had never been done before in the publishing industry for *Doctor Who*, and that is a series of nonfiction books that will have a continuity and be a dependable brand, which readers both new and old will be able to turn to for all things *Doctor Who*. Think of these books like a compendium. You will get tips on what to look for if you're deciding to watch the show for the first time. Maybe your friend is really into *Doctor Who*, and you want to find out what all the wibbly-wobbly timey-wimey stuff is all about. Maybe you've watched the show previously, but for whatever reason haven't been able to watch the 13th Doctor yet. Or maybe you've already watched Jodie's episodes before and are getting ready to binge watch the season again before Series 12 and are looking for anything you might have missed.

The plan is also to bring you content that has never been released, like exclusive interviews with people who contribute towards making *Doctor Who*, people who have drawn for The Doctor *Who* comics, written *Doctor Who* novels, worked for *The Doctor Who Magazine*, been part of their Time Team, and those who have dedicated their time towards running *Doctor Who* conventions worldwide.

What's more is that this book could not be happening at a more exciting time. This is a time where we are witnessing women demanding equal pay and opportunities that were once only promised to men. Women are becoming more dominant in the world where pop culture once presented women as submissive, unable to make their own decisions, and their property/worth belonging solely to men. It could be argued this change in pop culture began when Kate Mulgrew was cast as the first female captain in *Star*

Trek. We have also recently seen in comics where Captain America has become a woman, and now, our own *Doctor Who.* It is our honor to be able to contribute to this very place and time in pop culture. Which leads to another question. How do I fit into all of this?

* * *

In the late eighties, my local area went through what I'll call, "the dark ages." This meant *Doctor Who* wasn't being broadcast on television anymore and there wasn't anything new being made except for books from Target, Telos and Virgin, alongside some comics from Marvel and IDW.

By the time the revival of *Doctor Who* started in 2005, I had pretty much forgotten about The Doctor and his blue box. *The Lord of the Rings* had consumed my life with its books, movies, conventions, cosplay, collectibles, and more. In fact, it wasn't until about a decade later that I discovered my favorite show growing up had actually returned. And that was ironically also when I first started writing my young adult fantasy series, *The Rite of Wands.*

The Rite of Wands is about Mierta McKinnon, a 12-year-old wizard who has not yet gained his powers. He decides to undertake a ritual similar to the Christmas Carol, called *The Rite of Wands,* which shows him a vision of his past, present, and future. In his future, he sees something terrible happen to him and his family, so he decides to alter history so that event never happens.

Doctor Who Online, one of the first places I started networking with, endorsed my book, stating it was a "perfect mesh of *Doctor Who* and *Harry Potter*." That is when I started to realize that science fiction readers could find my fantasy novel just as appealing as fantasy readers, and maybe I needed to further re-evaluate my target audience decisions. Turns out, *Doctor Who* fans worldwide loved the book and practically made it a hit overnight. And that became further verified when I was able to hire Chris Walker-Thomson, who did an audio this year with Tom Baker for Big Finish Productions (*Doctor Who Comic Strip Adaptations: The Star Beast)*, to narrate my book.

One of the inspirations behind *The Rite of Wands*, which helped open doors to new networking opportunities for me that I don't take for granted for one minute, is the fact I wrote the main character of the series for actor Matt Smith, who played the 11th incarnation of The Doctor. That would never have happened had I not gotten back into *Doctor Who,* nor would I have had the fantastic opportunity to meet him briefly at Wizard World Chicago back in 2013, shortly before his departure from the show. It was the same convention, though a different year, where I met another author who represented the publisher with whom I would later sign a multi-book publishing contract.

Fast forward to 2017, I designed a wand for my series, which I honestly only meant to have as something cool to remember my series by and contacted the amazing Magical Alley to hand craft it for me. Coincidentally, around the same time it was going to be delivered, Matt Smith was scheduled to appear at Wizard World Cleveland which was near my parents' home. I decided to take a risk and brought it to Wizard World for Matt to sign. At the time he had no idea that *The Rite of Wands* even existed, and due to the limitations of comic con, I didn't have the opportunity to tell him, but he absolutely loved the wand and took the opportunity himself to swing it around and pretend to cast a spell on me. Later, I would learn that he had actually been originally cast to play Merlin in BBC's *Merlin*, but decided to go with *Doctor Who* instead.

A few months later, I learned he was going to be a guest at Fan Expo Canada, which is about a four-hour commute from my home. I decided to bring a copy of *The Rite of Wands* with me, as well as a letter telling him all about how he inspired my protagonist, because I knew I would have the same limitations as I did at Wizard World. Being that he isn't on social media, I knew staying in touch with him would be near impossible, but to my delight shortly afterwards his mother started following me on Twitter and has been one my biggest supporters.

Since then I have become an in-demand host and speaker for conventions in the United States such as Wizard World, Imaginarium LLC, Rochester Writers' Conference, Imaginarium Convention, Gallifrey One, Cleveland ConCoction, and MarCon. These conventions have helped me network and make friends with people who are connected with the actual show as well as Big Finish Productions. I can't picture what my life might be like had I not had *Doctor Who* as part of it, and it's through these connections that I envision bringing you all the insights and behind the scenes information about *Doctor Who* you could ask for!

CLASSIC DOCTOR WHO (1963-1989)

William Hartnell
First Doctor
Born: January 8, 1908
Died: April 23, 1975
First Appearance: November 23, 1963; age 55
Final Episode: October 29, 1966; age 58

Patrick Troughton
Second Doctor
Born: March 25, 1920
Died: March 28, 1987
First Appearance: October 29, 1966; age 46
Final Episode: June 21, 1969; age 49

Jon Pertwee
Third Doctor
Born: July 7, 1919
Died: May 20, 1996
First Appearance: January 3, 1970; age 50
Final Episode: June 8, 1974; age 55

Tom Baker
Fourth Doctor
Born: January 20, 1934
First Appearance: June 8, 1974; age 40
Final Episode: March 21, 1981; age 47

Peter Davison
Fifth Doctor
Born: April 13, 1951
First Appearance: March 21, 1981; age 29
Final Episode: March 16, 1984; age 32

Colin Baker
Sixth Doctor
Born: June 8, 1943
First Appearance: March 16, 1984; age 40
Final Episode: December 6, 1986; age 43

Sylvester McCoy
Seventh Doctor
Born: August 20, 1943
First Appearance: September 7, 1987; age 44
Final Episode: December 6, 1989; age 46

Paul McGann
Eighth Doctor
Born: November 14, 1959
Movie Appearance: May 14, 1966; age 36

MODERN DOCTOR WHO (2005-Present)

John Hurt
War Doctor (8.5)
Born: January 22, 1940
Died: January 25, 2017
One Episode: November 23, 2013; age 73

Christopher Eccleston
Ninth Doctor
Born: February 16, 1964
First Appearance: March 26, 2005; age 41
Final Episode: June 18, 2005; age 41

David Tennant
Tenth Doctor
Born: April 18, 1971
First Appearance: June 18, 2005; age 34
Final Episode: January 1, 2010; age 38

Matt Smith
Eleventh Doctor
Born: October 28, 1982
First Appearance: January 1, 2010; age 27
Final Episode: December 25, 2013; age 31

Peter Capaldi
Twelfth Doctor
Born: April 14, 1958
First Appearance: December 25, 2013; age 55
Final Episode: January 1, 2018; age 60

Jodie Whittaker
Thirteenth Doctor
Born: June 17, 1982
First Appearance: January 1, 2018; age 36

The Zeitgeist

"All of this is new to me. New faces, new worlds, new times. So, if I asked really, really nicely... would you be my new best friends?"
- 13th Doctor

Early 1963, Sydney Newman, the man responsible for helping create *Doctor Who*, was sitting in a meeting at the BBC discussing their Saturday evening programming. They were considering the idea of a new program to replace a half-hour classic literary adaptation show, which was suffering from very poor ratings at the time. Newman wasn't fond of classic literary adaptation shows and wished to follow the old BBC motto that broadcast programming was meant to "inform, educate and entertain." For him, that meant a new science fiction program featuring heroic figures.

"I love science fiction stories," Newman said, "because they're a marvelous way—and a safe way, I might add—of saying nasty things about our own society."

By April, C.E. Webber, who had written many successful BBC adaptations, wrote a pitch for the proposed program that he titled *Dr. Who*. For those already familiar with the show, what he suggested might be pretty surprising.

Webber describes *Doctor Who* as being about an old man lost in time and space. He's called *Dr. Who* simply because no one knows what the old man's name actually is, and he doesn't seem to remember where he came from either. All he knows is that he is searching for something, yet at the same time, running. He's suspicious, capable of doing bad things, and has an enemy not yet named. He hates scientists, inventors and improvers. People suspect he may be a criminal and/or may be lying about having lost his memory. The Doctor has a time machine, which allows him and companions—teachers Lola and Cliff—to travel through time, space and matter. *Doctor Who* is a mystery story, a quest story, containing the tale of this mysterious stranger. Webber would later add that authorities either from The Doctor's time or possibly even a future time, weren't so concerned about the time machine being stolen. They were more concerned The Doctor would either destroy or alter the future in a negative way.

While one can see the correlation between this pitch and the character development of The Doctor surrounding the events of the Time War (a war that haunts the various incarnations in the revived series), it goes quite against the grain of what *Doctor Who* is today! Newman didn't like the pitch and accused Webber of creating something that was absolutely *nuts*.

He wrote on the bottom of Webber's script: "I don't like this much—it reads silly and condescending. It doesn't get across the basis of teaching of educational experience—drama based upon and stemming from factual material and scientific phenomena and actual social history of past and future.

The mysterious Doctor should be a character who would take science, applied and theoretical, as being as natural as eating."

That is when the pitch changed to reflect how the show actually came about.

* * *

To describe the concept of *Doctor Who* to someone who has never seen the show before can be quite difficult; even honestly, a bit bonkers. When it comes down to the basics, it's about an alien from the planet Gallifrey, located in the Kasterborous constellation, who goes by the name The Doctor. But that's not their real name. The Doctor's real name is the biggest kept secret in *The Doctor Who* universe and only The Doctor's spouse will ever know their real name.

While they appear human, The Doctor is actually from a race called the Time Lords, who have been around far longer than humanity and have two hearts instead of just one. The first incarnation of The Doctor, played by William Hartnell, stole a time machine called the TARDIS and fled his home alongside his granddaughter, Susan. Together they landed in a junkyard on Totter's Lane where the two of them met history teacher, Barbara Wright, and science teacher, Ian Chesterton. These were the first of many companions that The Doctor would have over the years. The companions essentially representing the viewers, carrying them along across The Doctor's many adventures through time and space.

The TARDIS itself contains what the show calls a chameleon circuit, which allows it to alter its appearance to better camouflage with its surroundings. However, the chameleon circuit inside The Doctor's particular TARDIS is broken, leaving the time machine permanently stuck in the shape of a big, blue, British police box. If you've ever seen anything relating to Doctor Who, you're likely already familiar with how it looks!

The Doctor also carries a sonic screwdriver, which is kind of like science fiction's version of a magic wand without having to use words to cast spells. In fact, it looks nothing like an actual screwdriver, and is often times used to fix a problem or get out of a tough situation.

Scottish actor David Tennant, who portrayed the 10th incarnation of The Doctor, when asked about people's reactions to the show, said: "People love it and people of all generations love it. And even people who don't know it, love it. People who have never seen the show know they are supposed to love it, so they just love it. It's impossible to hate *Doctor Who*. It's full of love and it's expansive and it's embracing the universe quite literally."

* * *

There is no other show on the market like it. *Doctor Who* has been around for more than 50 years no doubt due in part to having such unique characteristics about it. The titular character, who has been portrayed by multiple different actors throughout the years, has been able to maintain a continuity throughout, partially due to the concept of regeneration. The thing about Time Lords is that when they die, they can come back with a new body. This concept was created when William Hartnell grew too ill to continue playing the part, but they didn't want to just replace the actor without explaining why his face suddenly looked different. And since then, we've had over a dozen actors play the part!

"Like The Doctor," said Dael Kingsmill, who has a video series on Greek Mythology on Felicia Day's *Geek and Sundry,* "the show is able to constantly reinvent itself and become the ultimate survivor. It's not constrained by time, or genre, or even cast, so it never gets old, but at the same time, it manages to hold onto that quirky quality which fans of the show know and love."

The show first premiered on November 23, 1963—the day after the death of legendary author C.S. Lewis, and the assassination of U.S. President J.F. Kennedy. This almost killed the show before it even began. Verity Lambert, the show's producer, implored the executives at BBC to rerun the first episode as most people were invested in watching news coverage of the events of the previous day. Fortunately for the show, the executives relented and reran the episode.

Believe it or not, *Doctor Who* was only supposed to run for one full year. Instead, what is now known as the classic series of *Doctor Who,* lasted for 26 years.

So, after all that time what caused the show to abruptly stop? The death bell for Classic *Doctor Who* began to ring in 1984 when a British broadcast executive, Michael Grade, became the Controller of BBC One. In 1985, he put the show on an 18-month hiatus, blaming low ratings, overly violent content, and absurd storylines as the cause. It was also noted that viewers were not connecting with Colin Baker's sixth incarnation of The Doctor. Many described his Doctor as abrasive, adding fuel to the flame as the BBC executives had already been discussing canceling the show.

Sydney Newman, along with Verity Lambert, wrote a letter in 1986 to Michael Grade, where he shared his thoughts on how to restore *Doctor Who* back to its former glory: "Something has to change. Colin Baker's second season is largely socially valueless, escapist schlock. At a later stage, *Doctor Who* should be metamorphosed into a woman. This requires some considerable thought—mainly because I want to avoid a flashy Hollywood 'Wonder Woman' because this kind of hero(ine) has no flaw—and a character with no flaws is a bore."

This was not the first time it was suggested the role of The Doctor could someday be played by a woman. When Tom Baker, who played the fourth incarnation of The Doctor, was asked about who his predecessor would be, he teased to the press that the fifth incarnation of The Doctor may be played by someone who was female. Fun fact: the fifth incarnation of The Doctor was supposed to be played by a woman! However, it never happened due to contract issues, and wasn't until now, almost 30 years later, that The Doctor's character would finally be a woman.

In 1986, Michael Grade was able to successfully convince John Nathan-Turner, the producer of the show, to fire Colin Baker. Michael's hope was to generate publicity for the series by doing something drastic, which Nathan-Turner was well-known for. Nathan-Turner then set out on a quest to find someone who could take on the role of The Doctor and had the ability to connect with the audience. That is when he decided on Sylvester McCoy for the part. Unfortunately, this was not drastic enough and the ratings continued to fall, leading to its inevitable cancellation in 1989, after transmitting 159 television stories divided among 695 episodes and one television special.

"I hated *Doctor Who*," said Grade. "I said to the producer, 'Do you go to the cinema much? Have you seen *Star Wars* or *ET*?' He said yes. I said, 'I've got news for you, so has our audience.' What we were serving up as science fiction was garbage."

However, that wasn't truly the end for *Doctor Who*. In 1996, the Fox network and BBC joined forces in order to attempt to revive the series by producing a single made for TV movie featuring an eighth incarnation of the character, played by actor Paul McGann. Will Brooks, known for his *Doctor Who* art, had created artwork for the movie, which, if the series had actually happened, would have had McGann portraying The Doctor for the next five years. Unfortunately, it was rejected.

Nonetheless, the movie ended up airing against one of the most popular prime time shows in the United States, *Roseanne*. The movie drew in a total of 9 million viewers in the UK while only bringing in a total of 5.5 million viewers in the United States. While the BBC was happy with the results, for it proved to them people were still invested in their *Doctor Who* brand, Fox was not, leading them to decline commissioning a new series. This left a hole that fans of *Doctor Who* felt needed to be filled. This hole led to books, comics, video games, and the creation of Big Finish Productions, which, to this day, continues to be successful in making audio dramas of *Doctor Who*, featuring actors from both the classic and the revived series.

Doctor Who finally returned back to the BBC and television screens in its revived series in 2005 with Christopher Eccleston as the ninth incarnation of The Doctor and Russell T. Davies as the new showrunner. The regeneration of the show explains that The Doctor is now the last of his kind, and that his people were killed during a Time War against another alien race known as the Daleks. With his home gone, he decided to continue traveling in his TARDIS, making friends, judging wrongs, and teaching values. He even, occasionally, became a hero.

Since the show's revival, *Doctor Who* has become successful not only in Britain, but also in Australia, and especially in America. It has won five consecutive awards at the National Television Awards (2005 to 2010) and received the 2006 British Academy of Film and Television Arts (BAFTA) award for best drama series. The show, even to this day, has been displayed on the cover of the *Radio Times Magazine* more often than any other science fiction show.

Looking back on being part of *Doctor Who* and the whole pop culture phenomenon, David Tennant, said in an interview with the Sag-Aftra Foundation: "It's amazing! It's amazing to be associated with something that people love so much. It's fantastic. It's such a privilege. It really is because I grew up watching that show and then it went away. You could argue that I became an actor because I fell in love with *Doctor Who*, but then it went away. But then it came back and then I got offered the part! It's all kind of sort of a bit mad, but wonderful to be a part of something when it was thriving and when it was being looked after by the geniuses that look after it now. Russell T. Davis just gets what television needs to be."

Despite all of the show's many accomplishments and successes, the one thing that has continued to plague behind the scenes in the revival of *Doctor Who* is controversy and drama.

* * *

In 2005, Christopher Eccleston, having been the ninth incarnation of The Doctor for only year, abruptly left without giving the press or the fans an explanation of why. One rumor reported that he left because of political reasons, due to the character of Captain Jack being gay. Another stated Eccleston had problems with the showrunner, while yet another stated it was because of typecasting. Whatever the reason, Eccleston appeared to shun The *Doctor Who* community, leaving the fans feeling confused, hurt, and questioning why. And when Eccleston turned down the opportunity to participate in the 50th anniversary episode in 2013, this further solidified the fans' beliefs that he didn't want anything to do with *Doctor Who*.

However, behind the scenes there was a whole different story going on. In his upcoming autobiography, *I Love the Bones of You*, Eccleston wrote that he struggled with mental illness and anorexia while filming *Doctor Who* while he was also helping to take care of his father who was suffering from dementia. "The illness is still there raging within me as The Doctor. People love the way I look in that series, but I was very ill. The reward for that illness was the part. And therein lies the perpetuation of the whole sorry situation."

And there was even more going on behind the scenes. Last year, Eccleston appeared in an article for *Radio Times* where for the first time he discussed what really happened between him, Russell T. Davies, Julie Gardner, Mal Young, and Phil Collinson: "What happened around *Doctor Who* almost destroyed my career," he said. "I gave them a hit show and I left with dignity and then they put me on a blacklist... I was told by my agent at the time: 'The BBC regime is against you. You're going to have to get out of the country and wait for regime change'. My relationship with my three immediate superiors—the showrunner, the producer and co-producer—broke down irreparably during the first block of filming and it never recovered."

He further explained the entire situation was very stressful and he felt out of place playing the role of a hero, because he had always played a villain. "Some of my anger about the situation came from my own insecurity," he continued. "They employed somebody as The Doctor who was not a natural light comedian. Billie Piper, who we know was and is brilliant, was very, very nervous and very, very inexperienced. So, you had that, and then you had me. Very, very experienced, possibly the most experienced on it, but out of my comfort zone."

When the 50th anniversary episode came around, he told fans at the Rose City Comic Con this summer that he liked Steven Moffat, who was the active showrunner, but was still expecting an apology from

BBC for how they had villainized him in the press in the past, which hurt him and his career, but never received it. He said that made him feel very depressed, and when he read the script, he didn't feel it would do his Doctor justice. So he declined, leading to the creation of a War Doctor to fill the role that had been written for his Doctor. For the record, he would have loved to have acted beside the late John Hurt.

Asked by a fan during his panel on why after all this time he is now starting to embrace *The Doctor Who* community again, Eccleston said:

"I think not one thing. I think there was a great deal of anger in me about the politics and the way I was treated in the aftermath. There was a lot of seriously bad politics by Russell and Julie and Phil and the BBC. I was officially blacklisted in the UK and didn't work for four years. So, what was so great for you guys wasn't so great for me. To a certain extent they needed to discredit me to help the next Doctor, and what they did was forgot I was a human being. I come from a place where we don't allow that kind of thing pass, but I've had children, I've had a nervous breakdown, I've gotten older. One thing I want to say to you is when you do theater or a premiere you will get autograph hunters. Like when I was doing *Macbeth*, you will get the same autograph hunters and they will want your autograph for the 100th or 150th time, and then they'll trade it or sell it and that means when you want to give your autograph for charity it's not worth as much because the internet is flooded, and that aggravated me and to be honest, I expected that at these kind of conventions, when it's the complete opposite. What I realized is you all do want to meet us, express your affection, and the memorabilia we sign is for you. These conventions are a very positive experience."

After the exit of Eccleston, the show hadn't been renewed for an additional series, nor had a replacement for The Doctor been found, putting the show's revival series at risk. David Tennant, while doing work with Russell T. Davies on the TV serial *Casanova,* was essentially and unknowingly auditioning for *Doctor Who.*

Because the series hadn't been renewed when Eccleston's Doctor regenerated into Tennant's, there was a strong possibility that *Doctor Who* could have ended after Tennant's Doctor smiled at Rose and recalled wanting to take her to Barcelona. Fortunately, the show was renewed, and David Tennant became one of the most popular actors to ever play The Doctor.

Then, a few years later in 2008, Tennant abruptly and emotionally announced live on ITV during the National Television Awards that he was leaving *Doctor Who*. "It would be very easy to cling on to the TARDIS console forever," he said to the audience. "I fear that if I don't take a deep breath and make the decision to move on now, then I simply never will." He would go on to film four *Doctor Who* specials before exiting the show in 2009 along with showrunner, Russell T. Davies.

However, we ALMOST saw a different version of series five of *Doctor Who*. Incoming showrunner,

Steven Moffat said in an interview with *DoctorWho.TV:* "David was just going through the—now, to me, very familiar—angst about leaving. I went to talk to David, and I ran him through what that series would be if it was him." Moffat went on to reveal what David's final series would have then been, before Tennant ultimately decided to follow through with his original decision.

"My version of that series would be that the David Tennant Doctor would crash into the back garden about to regenerate, and little Amelia Pond would help him back to the TARDIS and he'd fly off. Then she'd meet him again, when she grew up, but he'd have no memory of that because we come to realize that was The Doctor from the future—we'd make our way through the series to the point where The Doctor gets back to that."

So, now the new showrunner had a mission to find a new Doctor—someone who would have huge shoes to fill. Moffat originally envisioned a middle-aged actor, someone who could be old yet young at the same time, and even considered Peter Capaldi at one point, before he met Matt Smith.

Matt Smith, who would later be cast as the 11th incarnation of The Doctor, received a text message from his mother suggesting he should be the next Doctor. Later, his agent called him up to inquire if he would be interested in auditioning for the role. Like me, Matt grew up in the "dark ages" of *Doctor Who*, and in fact had never seen an episode of *Doctor Who*. However, because he was aware of how significant the science fiction show was in his country, he decided to audition.

"It's an iconic part of our culture. My granddad knows about it, my dad knows about it; it's been going since 1963. It has the iconic status of Robin Hood or Sherlock Holmes."

Ironically, Moffat met Matt for the first time at an audition for the role of Dr. Watson for the show *Sherlock*, another show he was showrunner for. When recalling the moment, Moffat said: "We'd already cast Benedict Cumberbatch as Sherlock Holmes and the very first person we saw for Dr. Watson was Matt, who came in and gave a very good audition. But he didn't have a chance in hell of getting it 'cos he was clearly more of a Sherlock Holmes than a Dr. Watson. There was also something a bit barmy about him—and you don't actually want that for Dr. Watson, you want someone a bit straighter. Oddly enough, I wrote an email where I said, 'I saw this guy today for Dr. Watson and I'd noticed he was on the list for *Doctor Who*—so The Doctor did flip through my head at that time."

What is also interesting about the timing of all this is the fact Matt was also up for the role of Merlin in BBC's *Merlin*, and had in fact won it. During a panel at the Two Doctors, a Wizard World New York special event that took place in 2014, Matt revealed he had been cast as Merlin, and Karen Gillan (who would go on to play his companion Amy Pond) had been cast as Genevieve. He had always wanted to be a wizard, but decided to do *Doctor Who* instead. That may not have happened had their agent not intervened. When Matt had called his agent to say he wasn't sure about doing *Doctor Who*, the agent informed him he WAS going to do it, which led to him signing the contract.

If that wasn't enough, Jodie Whittaker had in fact auditioned for a role in *Doctor Who* during Matt Smith's first series!

"I obviously didn't get it!" Whittaker laughed, when she chatted with *Radio Times* during the premiere of her first episode as the 13th Doctor. She admitted she didn't even remember exactly what role she had auditioned for. "I don't know if I was sent the whole episode script. I think I just put myself on tape, but I didn't get it. But thank goodness I sent some message-in-a-bottle tape and didn't get it, and then now... because I might have ruled myself out!"

Matt Smith's tenure as The Doctor didn't come without controversy however. He was the youngest person ever cast as The Doctor, and it is believed that the producers weren't convinced he could do the role justice. Even fans of *Doctor Who* were randomly yelling at him in the streets of UK not to screw up the show. Fortunately, he proved all the naysayers wrong, bringing *Doctor Who* to the largest audience in American and Australia to date.

Matt announced his departure from the role of The Doctor in 2013, which he now regrets because he wished he had had a full series with Jenna Coleman, who played another companion, Clara Oswald, aka the Impossible Girl:

Doctor Who has been the most brilliant experience for me as an actor and a bloke. That largely is down to the cast, crew and fans of the show. I'm incredibly grateful to all the cast and crew who work tirelessly every day, to realize all the elements of the show and deliver *Doctor Who* to the audience. Many of them have become good friends and I'm incredibly proud of what we have achieved over the last four years.

Having Steven Moffat as showrunner write such varied, funny, mind-bending and brilliant scripts has been one of the greatest and most rewarding challenges of my career. It's been a privilege and a treat to work with Steven, he's a good friend and will continue to shape a brilliant world for The Doctor.

The fans of *Doctor Who* around the world are unlike any other; they dress up, shout louder, know more about the history of the show (and speculate more about the future of the show) in a way that I've never seen before, your dedication is truly remarkable. Thank you so very much for supporting my incarnation of the Time Lord, number Eleven, who I might add is not done yet, I'm back for the 50th anniversary and the Christmas special!

It's been an honor to play this part, to follow the legacy of brilliant actors, and helm the TARDIS for a spell with 'the ginger, the nose and the impossible one.' But when ya gotta go, ya gotta go and Trenzalore calls. Thank you, guys. Matt.

Peter Capaldi, who would play the next incarnation of the character, was the first actor to be cast as The Doctor who had a significant work history both in front and behind the camera. Around the time of his casting he was portraying Cardinal Richelieu in the BBC show *The Musketeers,* as well as the role of a doctor from the World Health Organization in the Hollywood disaster film, *World War Z.* This led to speculation around the *Doctor Who* online fandom that Capaldi was the new Doctor simply because in the credits of the *World War Z* movie, his character appears as "WHO Doctor."

What was interesting about the 12th Doctor's casting is that Peter Capaldi was not a complete unknown in the *Doctor Who* world. As a boy, he wrote a letter to a *Doctor Who* fan club, suggesting storylines for the show. This led to him being invited to the BBC headquarters to meet those involved with the show. He even had been invited to audition for the role of the eighth Doctor, but decided not to audition because he was self-conscious, believing he wasn't good enough. However, he later appeared in a *Doctor Who* episode, *The Fires of Pompeii*, playing the role of sculptor Lobus Caecilius during David Tennant's era, as well as playing civil servant John Frobisher in the 2009 spin-off *Torchwood: Children of Earth*.

Despite the media attention Peter's casting received, there was also a lot of negativity. He was 55 years-old, which would have made him the same age as William Hartnell, yet fans in social media were stating that Capaldi was too old to play The Doctor. It was as though these fans were completely forgetting about the show's history.

During the time of the previous two Doctors, fans had fallen in love with the actors. They were young, handsome, and energetic. They were easy on the eye. Now you had an 'old guy' taking over the role. The fans felt betrayed. Their 'lover boys' had been replaced. No longer was The Doctor someone they could dream about meeting and marrying. No one wanted to hang a picture of Peter Capaldi on their bedroom walls.

What these young fans failed to realize is that The Doctor is a thousand-year-old alien who could change how he looked. The first four Doctors were portrayed by older men, and it wasn't until Peter Davison that The Doctor became younger. Casting Peter Capaldi as The Doctor was more a nod to the show's roots, showing the fans that anyone could be The Doctor!

I'll never forget the day I went to see the 50th Anniversary episode of *Doctor Who* and that first moment the audience got to see Peter Capaldi briefly as The Doctor. There is no way really to describe the feeling of hearing everyone in the theater literally cheer at the top of their lungs for Capaldi's cameo.

Steven Moffat admitted that he had planned to leave *Doctor Who* as showrunner at the same time as Matt Smith did but got so busy with the casting of the new Doctor, that he had decided to stay. This also gave him a reason to become excited again to write for *Doctor Who* during Capaldi's era. Unfortunately, despite starting out strong in Peter's era with 7.3 million viewers, by the time of their exits, the ratings had fallen to 5.5 million viewers. Some of this was caused by criticism of the writing and a one-year hiatus of *Doctor Who* in order for Moffat to be able to concentrate solely on the next series of *Sherlock,* although it was stated the show was put on hiatus due to the Olympics.

With the direct knowledge that Chris Chibnall would not accept the job of incoming showrunner without having the condition that the next Doctor be female, Capaldi decided to abruptly announce on a radio show that he was leaving the show due to health issues in 2017. It was something even the radio announcer was unprepared for.

"I want to always be giving it my best and I don't think if I stayed on, I'd be able to do that. I can't think of another way to say, 'This could be the end of civilization as we know it'."

With the uncertainty of who would be the new showrunner, the scriptwriters continued writing as they always had. The character of The Doctor was a male. Therefore, the early scripts were written for a male actor.

Then, on July 16, 2017, Doctor Who fans around the world experienced something that had never been done in the show before—The Doctor had become a woman, to be played by actress Jodie Whittaker.

And the achievements of *Doctor Who* didn't end there. In 2018, for the first time in the show's 55 year running history, episodes one through seven of its current series, made it during their respective weeks, into the Top 10 chart of the highest-rated programs.

* * *

The news of Jodie's casting wasn't all met with positivity. For example, Peter Davison shared with a live audience at the San Diego Comic Con his feelings about the casting: "If I feel any doubts, it's the loss of a role model for boys who I think *Doctor Who* is vitally important for. So, I feel a bit sad about that, but I understand the argument that you need to open it up. I prefer the idea of The Doctor as *a boy* but then maybe I'm an old-fashioned dinosaur—who knows?" Peter Davison would later be bullied off of Twitter by other fans in retaliation.

Colin Baker, who portrayed the sixth incarnation of The Doctor, disagreed with Peter Davison's comment, saying: "They've had 50 years of having a role model. So sorry Peter, you're talking rubbish there—absolute rubbish. Well, you don't have to be of a gender of someone to be a role model. Can't you be a role model as people?"

A certain minority of *Doctor Who* fans on social media started accusing the show of turning liberal and threatened to never watch the show again due to political correctness. That is when the famous #NotMyDoctor hashtag on Twitter began.

If only these fans had properly studied their history of the show, they would have known the choice to cast Jodie had nothing to do with politics. What it had to do with was the process of re-discovering what *Doctor Who* would ideally look like in 2018.

Before You Watch

*"Don't worry. I've got a plan... Well, I will have by
the time we get to the top."*
- 13th Doctor

When news broke out that a Roman Catholic school in
the state of Tennessee had banned J. K. Rowling's
magical Harry Potter series, after their pastor claimed
that the spells and curses contained within were not
only real, but had the capability of conjuring demons
simply by people reading the words, I posted on
Twitter stating sarcastically how I couldn't wait to
deal with this problem with *The Rite of Wands* series.
Most of my followers reacted to the article the way I
did; it was absurd and embarrassing. However, one of
my followers thought differently.

"Yes, they do," she said, referring to spells being
real. "They are evil."

I honestly thought she was being sarcastic. I mean,
if she really thought that, why was she following me? I
cannot count how many times I've posted about *The Rite
of Wands* on my feed, or a picture of me at a signing
where my banner even says the word *magical* on it.

"You don't really believe fantasy books
containing magic are evil, correct?" I wrote.

"Harry Potter is," she said before generalizing all fantasy books. "Yes, they are."

Again, I had to clarify. I really could not believe what I was reading.

"Can you please elaborate to this author who also writes books about magic why you think Harry Potter is evil?"

Next thing I knew, I had received a PM stating magic was evil before being blocked, preventing me from being able to discuss the topic with her further. I blinked a couple times, taking it all in, before coming to the conclusion that I had been talking with a "pudding-brain," a phrase to be used by the 12th incarnation of The Doctor when he was attempting to be insulting.

What the person's actions displayed was that she was not inclusive to anyone who wrote about magic, due to misinformation that magic in the books was real, and evil, and therefore anyone who wrote or practiced it was as well. Instead of getting the opportunity to properly educate her, I was judged based on the genre and story elements I write.

The above story is an example of the theme you'll find throughout Series 11 of *Doctor Who*, which, in this troubling time is super important—inclusivity and representation for all.

"*Doctor Who* celebrates change and inclusivity and regeneration, and that has to be for all," Jodie Whittaker said to the audience during a *Doctor Who* panel at New York Comic Con. "It can't just be for people that know it. The thing that The Doctor has taught me is that love and hope transcends time and space."

There were numerous thanks and congratulations from audience members, including one gentleman who shared his story of how he had to explain to his youngest daughter that despite society's rules that girls were supposed to like the color pink, she was permitted to like the color blue. She could be whatever she wanted to be, and he had helped her understand by using the 13th Doctor as an example. Jodie was very moved by the story.

Asked by an audience member if she had any advice for young girls and the women watching the show, Jodie said: "I think we have a voice. And we are entitled to be listened to. It's scary sometimes and we have to unite to have the bravery to use it, but let's use it. Also, we are flawed. Sorry, but we are, and that's a wonderful thing to embrace. Perfection is not the aim. It is too ironed out, like, the beauty and all the characters you love and cosplay as and/or, you know, meet in life, the characters you meet on the street. People are fascinating because of how different we are and much we shouldn't all be a clone. We are individuals, but on that, what is wonderful is a united hood, and what I can say for myself, the united sisterhood, but also the united 'Whovhood.' And the united humanhood that we can embrace and are embracing."

When Chibnall was asked if the theme of inclusivity is spread throughout Season 11, he replied: "This really comes down to what does *Doctor Who* look like in 2018. What does it look like for the next few years? It was about that on the writing team, directing team, in the edit suites, across the production and on the screen as well, yes. So, there is a lot of diversity in our casting and the stories we will tell will go places the show has never gone before in that sense and we'll tell stories that perhaps the show hasn't visited before."

Matt Strevens, the show's executive producer, added: "I think what's really important for us is that friends, which we used to call companions, are us; they are our POV. The Doctor is although the eponymous character, you see The Doctor, and the journey The Doctor takes you on, through the friends of The Doctor, so, it was really important to us and to Chris, that those friends represent everyone out there who's watching. They are just incredible and [so is] their joy of traveling with The Doctor."

Towards the end of the panel, Jodie discussed further about her Doctor, as well as revealed something that should make us all think: "The Doctor, particularly the way new showrunner Chris Chibnall has written her, is so full of hope and has that amazing ability to continually learn even with this extraordinary hindsight. And that's a life lesson, to never feel like you know the answer. And I think as adults we can often prejudge a scenario ... we're sometimes closed off to the openness of what could happen, and I think that's the opposite of The Doctor. That's an extraordinary thing to play."

* * *

One of the stories Chibnall refers to above can be found in episode three, titled *Rosa*, which features "the mother of the freedom movement," Rosa Parks. In the episode, The Doctor and her companions find themselves in 1955 Montgomery, Alabama, prior to the event when seamstress, Rosa Louise McCauley Parks, refuses to give up her bus seat to a white passenger. However, someone else is there from the future with a mission to stop this very important event in civil rights movement's history from ever happening.

"Rosa Parks might not be as familiar as some other figures in the civil rights movement, but she was incredibly important and that's why I was so keen to tell this story with a *Doctor Who* slant," explained Malorie Blackman during an interview with *Doctor Who Magazine*. "I did an awful lot of research into Rosa's life, but at the front of my mind I was telling a story about The Doctor and her companions. The episode is about the effect Rosa has on them and the effect they have on her."

"What I love about Rosa's story—and the way we're dealing with it in this episode," said Vinette Robinson, who portrays Rosa Parks. "It's got a real social conscience and powerful message to it. But we're telling it in a very engaging way. It's still fun; it's still *Doctor Who*."

"Real-life stories are very interesting dramatically, and to put them into *Doctor Who* is a very exciting collision," said Chibnall, who co-wrote the story with Blackman. "In *Rosa* our ensemble, our team, discover what it was actually like living in the period they're visiting… The joy of *Doctor Who*, the joy of being able to travel anywhere in space and time, is going to new places, meeting new people and seeing a story from their point of view. You can immerse your characters in that experience and tell historical stories in a different way from a documentary or a biopic. The series can introduce you to people you might not have learned about at school, or even if you did learn about them then, *Doctor Who* can show you a different facet or make you think about the story in a different way."

* * *

Another example of this year's *Doctor Who* theme is companion Ryan Sinclair's ongoing disability—dyspraxia, which we first learn about in the premiere episode when he is struggling to ride his bicycle. Dyspraxia is a developmental co-ordination condition affecting physical co-ordination. It causes a child to perform less well than expected in daily activities for their age, and appear to move clumsily.

"My nephew has dyspraxia, and I have friends with kids who also have dyspraxia. When we did a screening recently in Sheffield, there were a couple of journalists who approached me and said they also had dyspraxia. We worked with the Dyspraxia Foundation in the UK and talked to them. It was important, because people live with these things. It's a relatively common thing among kids. That's not an episodic story where it finishes at the end of that episode or for Ryan. It will carry on, it's a part of him, but there's also a lot of defining parts to Ryan, and that is one of them. I don't have the condition myself so I can't speak on it, but when we talk about heroes come in all shapes and sizes, that's what we mean," Chibnall said.

I was actually surprised to hear that this condition was quite common because at least where I live in the United States, I had never heard of the condition nor know anybody with it. Though what's interesting is I discovered through researching the condition that children with dyspraxia, 52% of them, according to the Dyspraxia Foundation, are also diagnosed with dyslexia. So, it's possible I DO know people who have it and they may not know it themselves.

Get to Know Your #TeamTARDIS

Name: Jodie Auckland Whittaker
Birthday: June 17, 1982
Birthplace: Skelmanthorpe, West Yorkshire, England, UK
Character: The 13th Doctor

What It Means Being in *Doctor Who*

"There is no other job in the world like this, where you can see so many different worlds, meet such amazing characters and speak such extraordinary dialogue. When it's all put together in one series, I hope it will blow the audience's minds as much as it blows mine when I read each new script."

On Playing 'The Doctor'

"As a young girl, I did not think that 'Time Lord' would ever be in my resume. I'm playing an alien and gender is not a part of that. A moment like this of being the first woman cast as something, it makes you really think about your sex, whereas actually what you want to do is play a part where your gender is irrelevant. I am a woman, so I don't need to play that. And so, for me, this was the most freeing experience because there's no right or wrong way to do it. The rules went out the window."

Did You Know?

She was named after the American actress, Jodie Foster.

On October 13, 2019—Jodie entered the Official Big Top 40 chart with a cover of Coldplay's iconic #Yellow at number 33.

She originally inquired with Chris Chibnall about playing a villain; He suggested she audition for the role of The Doctor, instead.

Name: Mandip Kaur Gill
Birthday: January 5, 1988
Birthplace: Leeds, West Yorkshire, England
Character: Yasmin Khan (Yaz)

What It Means Being in *Doctor Who*

"It literally means the world to me. The show is massive back at home. My brother-in-law is a huge fan. When I was auditioning, he said to me about a year ago, 'Man, if you get one episode of *Doctor Who*, I have to come.' And then… I'm a friend! I want to thank the fans for allowing the show to change so much and allowing new people to come on. I hope you enjoy, and I hope it means as much to you as it does to me."

Preparing for The Role

"I watched a lot of Jenna Coleman and Karen Gillan's stuff before and during the auditions because it's all easy to get hold of. I wanted to know how they were acting, so I didn't go into it too blind. And I watched some of Pearl's series because I wanted to see what went directly before me."

Did You Know?

She was a regular on the soap opera *Hollyoaks* with co-star Tosin Cole

She started acting at an early age, mostly performing for her family. With every performance, she received 50 pence.

She is a close friend of Jodie Whittaker

Name: Tosin Cole
Birthday: July 23, 1992
Birthplace: England
Character: Ryan Sinclair

What It Means Being in *Doctor Who*
"I'm happy to be on board on a so iconic show. It's something new for me and I'm looking forward to the journey and to experience it and see how you guys react to it."

Preparing for The Role
During the premiere of the first episode in Sheffield on September 24, 2017, Tosin revealed he had to be really bad at riding a bicycle due to his character having dyspraxia.

Did You Know?
He won the 2018 Saturn Award for Best Performance by a Younger Actor in a Television Series

He had a brief appearance in the film *Star Wars: The Force Awakens*, as the X-Wing pilot Lt. Bastian. His character gets to say, "Direct hit. No damage."

He has trouble keeping secrets.

Name: Bradley John Walsh—"Mr. Showbiz"
Birthday: June 4, 1960
Birthplace: Watford, Hertfordshire, England
Character: Graham O'Brien

On Playing Graham

"I try to play it as normally as possible so the reactions are pretty much how I would see them... The fact is this: you can never fully get to grips with time travel because we don't know what it's actually like... Graham's not trying to be the clown at all. He's just got that vernacular, bouncy humor which is naturally funny."

Preparing for The Role

During the premiere of the first episode in Sheffield on September 24, 2017, Bradley revealed he was required to wear a wig for the entire series, due to Graham being a lot older than he was.

Did You Know?

He appeared in two episodes of the *Doctor Who* spin-off *The Sarah Jane Adventures.*

At the age of 18, Walsh became a professional football player, but had to quit by age 22, due to ankle injuries.

His debut album, *Chasing Dreams*, became the biggest-selling debut album by a British artist in 2016, selling 111,650 copies.

He, Paul McGann and Peter Capaldi were in a film they made together in 2001 called *Hotel!*

Enemies to Watch For

Charlie Duffy

First appears in the episode—*Kerblam!* He is a maintenance worker at Kerblam, which is a galaxy-wide online shopping service consisting of automated warehouses, and a mostly robotic workforce known as TeamMates. Charlie is against robots taking jobs away from people and has a deadly plot to stop them.

Daleks

The Doctor's greatest enemy. They first appeared in *Doctor Who* back in 1963. They are extra-terrestrial cyborg mutants encased in a shell, which are incapable of love. They seek universe domination and will kill any species that they believe inferior and/or standing in their way to victory. They appear in the episode—*Resolution*, which was a New Year's special and the only episode of *Doctor Who* to air in 2019.

Gathering Coils

First appears in the episode—*The Woman Who Fell to Earth*. The Doctor describes them as a semi-species. They appear as a mass of electrical tentacles in order to gather information. They can also be used as a bio-weapon by having their coils micro-implant DNA bombs into their victims' bodies, targeting their genetic material groundwork and destroy it upon detonation. Tzim-Sha uses them to identify his prey in his specie's hunt.

Krasko

First appears in the episode—*Rosa*. He's a previously convicted murderer who was imprisoned in the Stormcage Containment Facility, who has obtained a vortex manipulator, allowing him to time travel. He has a deep hatred for African Americans and is determined to nullify key events that took place in the civil rights movement.

Manish

Younger brother of Prem, who the audience meets in the episode—*Demons of the Punjab*. He opposes the wedding between Prem and Umbreen, Yasmin's grandmother.

Morax

First appears in the episode—*The Witchfinders*. An alien prison, which was disguised as a tree, has been cut down, and now is unable to keep Morax war criminals at bay. Those who have escaped plan to possess King James and take over the Earth.

Mutated Earth Spider

These genetically modified spiders are offspring of one that was created by US businessman Jack Robertson's company, which mutated further after a coal mine was filled with his company's waste. Throughout the history of *Doctor Who*, numerous Doctors have encountered enlarged spiders.

Pting

First appears in the episode—*The Tsuranga Conundrum*. What appears at first to look like an extra-terrestrial from the universe of Disney's *Lilo and Stitch*, the Pting are vicious, non-carnivorous bipedal creatures, interested in eating inorganic materials, which required energy.

Solitract

First appears in the episode—*It Takes You Away.* It is an exiled entity with capabilities to be able to experience seeing and feeling sensations that are contradictory with our universe. The Solitract became its own universe and is seeking companionship.

Tzim-Sha

First appearing in the episode—*The Woman Who Fell to Earth*, Tzim-Sha is a warrior from a species called Stenza. He comes to the planet Earth in a pod, which he waits in until someone activities the Gathering Coils. The Stenza live in an environment whose temperature is far below Earth's, making anyone who touches their skin die instantly. He is called "Tim Shaw" by the Doctor after mishearing his name.

Voice of the Remnants

First appears in the episode—*The Ghost Monument.* They can smell the Doctor's fear and desire to feed on it.

New Accessories

The 13th Doctor's TARDIS

Since the show's beginning, the TARDIS has been the Doctor's consistent companion. While her interior has drastically changed over the years, her exterior has for the most part remained the same. However, that can no longer be said to be true.

During Peter Capaldi's reign, the BBC confirmed the official blue color paint of the TARDIS was Pantone 2955C. However, Jodie Whittaker's TARDIS looks weathered unlike the fresh colored paint look of Peter Capaldi's TARDIS. But, that's just the beginning of the TARDIS's changes:

The St. John Ambulance Logo is gone—to keep the authenticity of the blue police box, the TARDIS had a St. John Ambulance logo on the right door. However, that logo, for Series 11 has been removed.

The instruction sign—One of the most characteristic features of the TARDIS is the instruction sign, which can be found on the left door. Though it has varied by size and color, it's most known for being black lettering on a white background. In fact, the last time fans saw the instruction sign colors inverted, meaning the instruction sign has white lettering on a black background, was during the 1996 movie. Now, nearly 20 years later, the inverted instruction sign is back!

New interior—The TARDIS's new interior strangely matches the new sonic screwdriver with what appears to be Stenza technology, which that in itself, I find a bit strange.

The Doctor's Costume

The 13th Doctor's new costume is a collaboration between Jodie Whittaker and Ray Holman, who also helped design the 11th Doctor's costume. As part of the collaboration, Ray Holman asked Jodie if he could add a violet lining (which is more of a pink violent) inside the sleeves, which she agreed to. Jodie was inspired by a photograph from a 1988 issue of *Sassy*, where females were modeling men's clothing.

"Throughout my audition process, I sent Chris probably an image a day from something, somewhere. I loved the energy of this one black and white image of a woman walking with purpose and deep in thought with cut trousers, boots, braces and a T-shirt," said Jodie Whittaker to the New York Comic Con audience. "And because it's black and white you can't tell where it's from, but it has the fun element of a T-shirt and it has the timelessness of a pleat in a trouser-like. If you look back at it, and held the image of it far away, it was genderless, and obviously that person could move in it and it was comfortable. And because it was black and white, it didn't give it mood, it was there to be created for us. So, that was our starting off point.

And then the coat, I loved the coat. I loved the coat so much! But the coat and the conversations about colors and use of color because I'm quite a colorful character. I like color and I think I wanted to reflect the moments of brightness that would be, but in the coat, the interior lining is dark blue and I felt that it represented the space I was following through in the episode, *The Woman Who Fell to Earth,* and then the exterior is like a dawn sky, and it has the important things, it has a pocket, it has more than one. It has without me spoiling it, every single stitch has a meaning and every single piece of cut and lining."

A Word of Caution For Cosplayers

If you, a family member or friend wishes to cosplay as the 13th Doctor, be extra cautious of the retailers who claim to sell an accurate edition of the coat, or you could regret ending up looking like I did at Gallifrey One!

The New Sonic Screwdriver

Not all heroes require weapons and The Doctor is definitely one character you won't see carrying them. She would rather outwit and outlast her opponents using her brain, but even sometimes she needs a little bit of extra help in order to get out of a sticky situation.

For the first time in the show's history, The Doctor gets to create her own sonic screwdriver, rather than requiring the need to obtain one from the TARDIS. One could argue the sonic has become as legendary of an item as the TARDIS itself. This new sonic is constructed of Sheffield steel and a glowing orange crystal from an alien's ship, which simply emphasizes how brilliant the 13th Doctor really is.

The 13th Doctor sonic was a design collaboration between Arwel Wyn Jones *(Doctor Who* Production Designer) and Darren Fereday (*Doctor Who* Concept Artist). It was crafted by Nick Robatto, who is the master prop-master of *Rubbertoe Replicas*, in the company's workshop versus a garage in Sheffield.

The sonic is cast with pewter versus a cold-cast resin or a painted finish. It took Robatto initially two weeks to make the first 13th Doctor sonic, using at least 50 components from various materials. You can purchase an actual replica of the sonic from *Rubbertoe Replica's* website, along with 11's and 12's sonics, but it will cost you $916.27 plus the cost of shipping and taxes.

The Doctor's Scarf

In the only 13th Doctor episode to air in 2019, the audience had the pleasure of seeing the Doctor in a new multi-colored scarf. While she has only worn it thus during that episode, it is a piece all 13th Doctor cosplayers have been eagerly waiting to get their hands on. And, good news, now you can!

The scarf was originally designed by Paul Smith, made with high quality Merion wool in screen accurate colors of teal, navy and a bright pink accent line. For those who are cosplayers and absolutely have to have this authentic scarf, it is available to purchase for $130 on the Paul Smith's website.

A new officially licensed scarf has been announced by *Lovarzi*, which can be purchased through their website. Their scarf is made with Soft Acrylic. It was inspired by the 13th Doctor's rainbow shirt, so, because the original design is copyrighted by Paul Smith, the scarf is not screen accurate.

How/Where to Binge

Classic Doctor Who
Pluto TV
Britbox

Current Doctor Who
AMC
HBO Max (spring 2020—will be exclusive)
Amazon Prime
BBC America app
iTunes
Google Play
Xbox
Vudu
Microsoft

Episode Guide

"There's this moment, when you're sure you're about to die, and then... you're born. It's terrifying. Right now, I'm a stranger to myself. There are echoes of who I was and a sort of call towards who I am. And I have to hold my nerve and trust all these new instincts, shape myself towards them."
- 13th Doctor

This chapter is where I shall break down each episode of Series 11, give you some behind-the-scene insights, and share what my personal feelings were as I watched them. After all, *Doctor Who* really is "one big ball of wibbly-wobbly, timey-wimey... stuff". Right? Let's get a shift on!

Episode 1: The Woman Who Fell to Earth
Aired: October 7, 2018

Network	BBC One
Writer	Chris Chibnall
Director	Jamie Childs
Producer	Nikki Wilson
Executive Producer(s)	Chris Chibnall, Matt Strevens, Sam Hoyle
Cast	Jodie Whittaker (13th Doctor), Bradley Walsh (Graham O'Brien), Tosin Cole (Ryan Sinclair), Mandip Gill (Yaz)
Guest Cast	Sharon D Clarke (Grace), Samuel Oatley (Tim Shaw), Jonny Dixon (Karl), Amit Shah (Rahul), Asha Kingsley (Sonia), Janine Mellor (Janey), Asif Khan (Ramesh Sunder), James Thackeray (Andy), Philip Abiodun (Dean), Stephen MacKenna (Dennis), Everal A Walsh (Gabriel)
Rating	10.96m
Fun Fact	Jodie Whittaker did her own stunts!

The audience is introduced to the newly regenerated Doctor, played by Jodie Whittaker, who has literally fallen from the sky. She crashes through the roof of a train, landing in front of a group of frightened people from Sheffield. She soon discovers the train has been stopped by some kind of alien threat. The Doctor, with no TARDIS, no weapons, and empty pockets, must join the group of stranded people in order to unravel the mystery of this new alien attack before coordinating a plan to save everyone from danger.

REVIEW

It's hard to believe that as I'm writing this portion of the chapter, we're only six more days away from the anniversary of when this episode, *The Woman Who Fell to Earth*, first aired on October 7, 2018! I remember preparing for this episode with mixed feelings. I was excited to see more of Jodie's Doctor, yet I was sad because we would no longer be able to enjoy seeing Capaldi's Doctor in fresh new episodes.

This is something all Whovians experience when one actor leaves the leading role and is inadvertently replaced by another. It honestly feels like, as a fan, you're going through the five stages of grief. First you're sad, because you've lost "your Doctor" and some stranger has now suddenly replaced him or her. You feel like *they*, even though they really didn't, "killed" the Doctor. Without being fair, you move towards becoming furious, thinking that this new actor is totally going to ruin the show and everything *Doctor Who* stands for (*Thanks for destroying my childhood*, may be simply one of the things that will go through your head!)

Looking back, Jodie Whittaker had a lot of pressure stepping into the role of the 13th Doctor. Her first episode would be considered historical because it involved the leading character, the Doctor, becoming female for the first time in *Doctor Who's* 50 plus year history. She not only had to prove to the naysayers that a woman could be just as capable at handling a sonic screwdriver and the infamous TARDIS as well as a man, but she had to show the Doctor's new gender was uneventful to the storytelling. The question would end up being, would she be able to pull it off? Was the hype all worth it?

That answer is, YES! Jodie Whittaker and her Doctor couldn't have had a better episode to welcome her officially into the *Doctor Who* family.

The last time the audience was with the Doctor, Peter Capaldi (the 12th incarnation of the character, an older white-haired Scottish man) was in the process of regenerating into the Doctor's 13th incarnation, now being played by actress Jodie Whittaker. There was just enough time for her to see her reflection in the mirror, realize this new regeneration was female, and delightfully say, 'Oh, Brilliant!' before the TARDIS abruptly, and rudely I might add, tossed her out. The show left us watching as she fell rapidly down to Earth, before the TARDIS exploded and dematerialized in the night sky.

The audience was left to wonder—is it because the TARDIS no longer recognizes her as the Doctor? Is this Chibnall's way of poking fun at the fans who are part of the #NotMyDoctor movement, who display downright hatred for Jodie Whittaker with their misogynistic behavior and have declared that the Doctor can't be a female? Or, was the TARDIS simply trying to save the Doctor's life from the oncoming explosion?

In America, this episode was advertised to be broadcast simultaneously between the US and the UK, but that quickly became untrue. While the episode was broadcast in its entirety in the UK without ads, America's television broadcast did have ads, which resulted in the episode running an entire hour longer. British fans were also permitted to listen to the show's new theme song. However, in America, there was a preview ad running over it causing US fans to have to wait an extra week before they could enjoy the new theme.

The 13th Doctor is like a breath of fresh air. She's quirky, energetic, and perhaps a bit bonkers because she has absolutely no memory of what her name is, and is visibly shaken after crash landing literally through the roof of a train. The audience only has to spend a few minutes with this Doctor before she throws a perfect impersonation of Capaldi as her Doctor starts to display her inner turmoil of having lost her TARDIS, sonic screwdriver, has a coat with empty pockets, and is stuck with a body and mind that is still rebooting/reformatting.

Chibnall had instructed Jodie not to watch any prior episodes of *Doctor Who*, so that she would not be influenced by any actor in the role previously and make the role of the Doctor her own. To pull off such a spot-on impersonation is kudos to the directing team.

"I wanted to read my research, not watch it," Jodie said to *Yahoo Movies* at a special premiere of the first episode in Sheffield. In preparation for the role, she added that she didn't want to feel "bound in" by too much knowledge of how others had played it. "You question yourself a lot as an actor, and I never wanted to third eye it and think: Has this been done before? Am I trying to be like someone else, or is this me in the moment?"

Chibnall has managed to successfully bring *Doctor*

Who into the 21st century by way of technology. *Doctor Who*, due to budget restraints, has never looked as good as a made for series shot for Netflix. However, the cinematography is absolutely gorgeous and can be immediately noticed when aerial shots are seen from Garth Mountain.

Chibnall's writing is also very different from previous showrunners. Both Moffat and Davies tended to build their series around story arcs and lots of frightening monsters that could cause smaller children to have nightmares, while Chibnall liked individual episodes similar to how classic *Doctor Who* was constructed. While it would be unfair to base his writing off of one episode, I'll be honest, I haven't cared for any of his previous episodes, so I really wasn't expecting a lot. Yet, his writing on the drama and mystery series, *Broadchurch*, was absolutely spectacular! Could the problem simply be writing comedy?

Fortunately, these fears are quick to dissolve. Loyal viewers of the show could expect to hear typical lines from the Doctor, like, 'That's exciting!' when encountering something new, but instead, Chibnall throws in a surprise and abruptly has the Doctor add to that line: "No, not exciting. What do I mean? Worrying." It's something different, which makes it satisfying.

This series has also been promised to be different than any other. We are to hear from voices we have never heard from before to fulfill Chibnall's goal of bringing *Doctor Who* into the 21st century, with themes of inclusiveness and representation for all.

This theme can be seen all the way down to the Doctor's new coat and rainbow striped shirt. It's rather a shame that the audience only gets to see her in the new costume nearly at the end of the episode when Yaz makes a comment she should get out of the Time Lord's former coat, not to mention how it must have smelled by this point.

The audience isn't going to see classic monsters like the Cybermen or scary monsters like the Weeping Angels this time around. That's already apparent when we get to see the Doctor craft her own sonic screwdriver instead of relying on the TARDIS. She also runs into one of the creepiest characters I have seen on the revival of *Doctor Who*, Tzim-Sha of the Stenza, who has human teeth sporadically arranged on his face. She also gets to battle a Gathering Coil, which is like this gigantic ball of multiple snake-like tentacles, there for the sole purpose of gathering information to assist Tzim-Sha in his hunt for a crane operator, Karl. An interesting fact about Tzim Sha is that his character was originally meant to die in this episode when Karl kicked him off the crane. But Chibnall changed his mind and decided to revive him for the episode with the Ux.

Another notable change is the number of travelers aboard the TARDIS. Traveling along with the Doctor in this series, we have Graham O'Brien, who is like the grandpa of the group; Ryan Sinclair, a 19-year-old African American boy who suffers from dyspraxia; Yazmin Khan, another 19-year-old who is training to become a police officer; and for the first episode, Grace, who is Ryan's Nan and Graham's wife. Bradley Walsh, who plays companion Graham O'Brien, had to wear a wig during this series because the show wanted him to look older since Graham was older.

Jodie also stated in an interview with *Doctor Who Magazine* that this episode was particularly challenging to shoot because it was cold and raining during most of their time filming. She also performed her own stunts for this episode. Jonny Dixon, who played Karl, requested to perform his own stunts, and when Jodie found out she told everyone she was going to do her own too. It was especially thrilling, yet nerve wracking, for the crew to watch them perform their own stunts from 50 feet in the air in harnesses! However, this was the only episode Jodie was permitted to perform without her stunt double.

The last significant change to mention is the musical composer, Segun Akinola. He brings more of a cinematic emotional ambient sound to Series 11 which is different from Murray Gold's easily recognizable style of music, completing Chibnall's vision of bringing *Doctor Who* to 2018.

One thing I missed from my first viewing of *The Woman Who Fell to Earth* was the newspaper in the warehouse, with a headline that read, 'Strange Sighting in Skies Over Sheffield.' It was only then that I realized the owner of the warehouse was kind of like *Smallville*'s Chloe Sullivan, but a bit like Mulder from *X-Files*, trying to solve the mystery of what happened to his sister.

Here's another thing I missed. How many of you spotted the ceramic frog in front of Grace's photograph on Ryan's desk? Seeing that, makes what occurs in *It Takes You Away* seem not so ridiculous now. Seriously, go back and watch. You now have your first Easter egg!

Overall this episode completely lived up to its hype, blew my mind away, and I'm looking forward to what Chibnall and the rest of the writing team has in store for us the rest of this series.

Episode 2: The Ghost Monument
Aired: October 14, 2018

Network	BBC One
Writer	Chris Chibnall
Director	Mark Tonderai
Producer	Nikki Wilson
Executive Producer(s)	Chris Chibnall, Matt Strevens, Sam Hoyle
Cast	Jodie Whittaker (13th Doctor), Bradley Walsh (Graham O'Brien), Tosin Cole (Ryan Sinclair), Mandip Gill (Yaz)
Guest Cast	Susan Lynch (Angstrom), Shaun Dooley (Epzo), Art Malik (Ilin), Ian Gelder (Voice of the Remnants)
Rating	9m
Fun Fact	Tosin Cole suffered heat stroke during filming

While attempting to lock onto the TARDIS's last known coordinates in the galaxy, the 13th Doctor accidentally transports herself as well as her new companions—Graham, Ryan and Yaz, to a planet that has fallen out of orbit. They are rescued by aliens who are on an intergalactic race towards their final destination, the planet of Desolation. Becoming part of the race, too, the Doctor and her friends seek out the finish line—the Ghost Monument.

REVIEW

After the 13th Doctor's brilliant crash-landing into Sheffield, the second episode picks up directly where the show last left her; free floating in space after she had locked on to what she thought was the coordinates of her missing TARDIS. She opens her eyes, looks around and you can see the shock form on her face as she realizes what a potentially tragic mistake has taken place. She sees that Ryan, Graham, and Yaz have been teleported along with her.

Viewers will be transported to a world that previous *Doctor Who* fans might say feels more like the show they know. There are various science fiction elements, including robots, spaceships, oh, and did I mention, a post-apocalyptic environment? The world they end up on is absolutely barren.

Welcome to Desolation, a once flourishing world, now reduced to desert and wasteland. It's the site for the last leg of an alien intergalactic version of a reality show like *The Amazing Race,* called 'Rally of the Twelve Galaxies,' which the Doctor and her friends are forced into when they find themselves aboard the ships of the last two competitors. The prize for finishing the race is life-changing for the winner. We slowly learn the back stories of the competitors throughout the episode.

Angstrom is an Albarian female participant who claims that she joined the race in desperation. Her family went into hiding when their planet was attacked by an alien race. If she wins the race, she plans to find her family and relocate them somewhere that they will be safe and able to live in peace. Epzo is a Muxteran male participant, he seems to be interested in nothing more than his own comfort. He relates a story where his mother made him climb a tree as high as he possibly could, then told him to jump. She reassured him that she would catch him. She didn't. He ended up with a broken arm and ankle. The lesson he learned? He can never trust anyone.

This episode was the first in the history of *Doctor Who* to be filmed in South Africa. Showrunner, Chris Chibnall said he chose this site because it provided the best environment for "The Ghost Monument" story. One problem that the cast and crew faced was a drought. It was extremely hot and extremely dry. Tosin Cole, who plays companion Ryan Sinclair, experienced heatstroke during the filming of this episode. Chibnall said that the cast could not film without taking showers every two minutes.

With every new Doctor comes a new theme song. Remember with the 12th Doctor it had a distinct 'rock' feel to it? Well this series is no different. For this one the audience gets to hear the new composer, Segun Akinola's, interpretation of the show's theme; an absolutely delightful rendition that mixes classic with modern. It had previously been reported in *Radio Times* that a sample of the original 1963 version of the series theme had made it into this creation.

"I really just stuck to the original theme," said Akinola, "like the very, very first one, and tried to glean as much from that as I could from it. I tried to honor the original theme as much as I could as well. It's such an iconic theme, one that people walking down the street can whistle, and it's one that people really care about as well. Our viewpoint across the whole thing was basically that it should be new—but new didn't mean that it had to be the opposite of everything that has come before. It was really just a blank slate, an opportunity to look at it and start again. There wasn't anything that I particularly tried to avoid in any grand way. I just tried to make it the best it could be."

There's also a new enemy, born out of the destruction of Desolation, with a super creepy way of attacking its enemy. It creeps into their minds and reveals their deepest secretes and regrets. It was created in a lab by the long dead scientists of this desolate land who were forced to create it by a surprise entity. They appear to be nothing more than rags. But these rags are self-aware and able to think and speak. These entities, called The Remnants, get into The Doctor's mind and, in doing so, brings forward an important message to the Doctor. They called her *the Timeless Child*. This message may end up being used for a story arc at a later date, but for now, is merely a tease for the viewing audience. I will say I do hope they expand on this message.

This episode represents the best reflection of the Doctor's character. There is noteworthy character development for the 13th Doctor. The audience gets a glimpse of what kind of Doctor she really is and most importantly, her morals. This will ultimately lead towards conflict between the companions, specifically, Ryan, as he begins to question whether the Doctor is truly trustworthy.

There is also use of witty humor by the 13th Doctor in this episode when she refers to a time when she was a hologram and heard lots of gossip. It's possible this may have been referring to a time when the 11th Doctor briefly became a hologram in the Titan Comics. There may be other references to the Titan Comics throughout this series. Who knows? We shall have to watch and see.

Towards the end of the episode, when everyone has reached the finish line, the site of the Ghost Monument, the Doctor and her companions are abandoned on the Planet Desolation by the moderator of the race much to the chagrin of the competitors. Here, when all seems lost, the TARDIS miraculously appears. The Doctor looks on in awe as the TARDIS is trying to materialize. She even coaxes it on saying, "Come on my beautiful ghost monument, come to Daddy, I mean Mummy." The viewing audience is treated to a new interior design and the Doctor is treated to her new favorite, a custard cream biscuit.

When Jodie was first introduced to the new TARDIS interior by production designer, Arwel Jones, she was blown away. She was also not instructed how to drive the TARDIS, for each actor who has portrayed the Doctor has had his or her own way of piloting it. Instead, the director said they would follow her. Jodie genuinely did not know there was a station that made custard cream biscuits, so when the viewing audience sees her Doctor's reaction, that is a legit surprise.

While this episode was not able to satisfy my expectations after the jaw dropping opening series' episode, it is early in the 13th Doctor's era and one that should not be missed.

Episode 3: Rosa

Aired: October 21, 2018

Network	BBC One
Writer	Malorie Blackman and Chris Chibnall
Director	Mark Tonderai
Producer	Nikki Wilson
Executive Producer(s)	Chris Chibnall, Matt Strevens, Sam Hoyle
Cast	Jodie Whittaker (13th Doctor), Bradley Walsh (Graham O'Brien), Tosin Cole (Ryan Sinclair), Mandip Gill (Yaz)
Guest Cast	Vinette Robinson (Rosa Parks), Joshua Bowman (Krasko), Trevor White (James Blake), Richard Lothian (Mr. Steele), Jessica Claire Preddy (Waitress), Gareth Marks (Police Officer Mason), David Rubin (Raymond Parks), Ray Sesay (Martin Luther King), Aki Omoshaybi (Fred Gray), David Dukas (Elias Griffin Jr), Morgan Deare (Arthur)
Rating	8.41m
Fun Fact	Vinette was offered the role of Rosa Parks without an audition

While attempting to get her friends back safely home to Sheffield, the Doctor and her friends accidentally travel to 1955 Alabama where they discover traces of artron energy, and a racist time traveling criminal named Krasko attempting to prevent one of the most historic figures in the American civil rights movement, Rosa Parks, from refusing to give up her seat.

REVIEW

In the third episode of Series 11, when attempting to return back to Sheffield, the Doctor and her friends find themselves taking a detour in the TARDIS to the city of Montgomery located in the state of Alabama, part of the United States of America, in the year 1955. There, they discover the TARDIS has transported them to the day before a key event of the American civil rights movement, where Rosa Parks refuses to give up her seat on a segregated city bus. Except this time there is an additional threat; a threat that could change the course of history if the Doctor and her companions cannot find a way to stop it, first.

This isn't the first time the TARDIS has taken the Doctor to a different destination than what was originally intended. The TARDIS does have a mind of its own, as many long-time fans have surmised. It has a way of taking the Doctor where he/she *needs* to be rather than where he/she *wants* to be. It's also not the first time an historical figure has appeared in an episode of *Doctor Who*. We've had appearances from Hitler, Queen Elizabeth I, Queen Victoria, Churchill, and Shakespeare, just to name a few.

The episode opens with an event in the year 1945,

after the state of Alabama has passed a law requiring all bus companies under its jurisdiction to enforce segregation. It is ironic because most of the passengers at that time were African American due to the fact most whites could afford cars, eliminating their need to use public transportation. This is the same year seamstress, Rosa Louise McCauley Parks, is also abruptly set off a bus by driver, James Blake, introducing the audience to the conflict of racial discrimination that is beginning to unfold.

In 1946, the Montgomery NAACP was beginning to think they should file suit against the city of Montgomery over bus segregation, except they had not found the right candidate yet. Their ideal plaintiff would be a woman, because she would get more sympathy than a man, with a good reputation and who would have done nothing wrong except refusing to give up her seat. That almost happened in the year 1955 when a teenage girl by the name of Claudette Colvin in the spring of that year refused to give up her seat. However, she was later dismissed as the ideal plaintiff when it was discovered she was pregnant and unmarried.

Fast forward to the summer of the same year. The audience encounters Rosa Parks again after the Doctor's companion, Ryan Sinclair, attempts to return an item that was dropped by a white woman, only to get a slap in the face from her husband as a thank you. Rosa is able to intervene before anything worse happens, and the Doctor and her friends are able to convince everyone else they are out-of-towners. Rosa warns them to be careful because she doesn't want to see Ryan become the next Emmett Till. Emmett Till was a 14-year-old boy from Mississippi who was lynched after being accused of flirting or whistling at a white woman in late summer 1955.

While the Doctor and her companions are taking in the excitement of having just met a person of history, the Doctor suspects there is something more going on. Her theory is proven correct when she discovers Rosa Parks has traces of artron energy from what the Doctor believes could only be from another time travel device. They decide to trace the artron energy to find its origins, which leads them to a suitcase in a warehouse. There, they meet its owner, where he attempts to zap them with a time displacement device before they are able to investigate what's inside the suitcase. The Doctor concludes he is there to prevent Rosa Parks from refusing to give up her seat and instructs her friends to learn all they can before the critical event.

Interestingly enough, the real Rosa Parks wrote in her book *My Story* that she would not have even gotten on that bus on the evening of December 1, 1955 if she had actually been paying attention. Most of the time when she had seen Mr. James Blake, whose name she also didn't know until she saw him later in court, driving the bus, she would automatically not even bother getting on. She also didn't know whether he had been on that particular route before because the bus company would switch the drivers around sometimes.

However, Rosa was way more preoccupied with getting together a workshop for the NAACP that was supposed to be taking place on December 3rd and 4th. She had also been attempting to get the consent of Mr. H. Council Trenholm at Alabama State to have the meeting at the college, but she was having a very difficult time simply getting his consent. Plus, she was also getting the notices in the mail for the elections of officers of the Senior Branch of the NAACP. It's no wonder she wasn't paying attention to who was driving the bus!

Later, the Doctor returns to the warehouse and confronts the time traveler whom we learn is a racist named Krasko. He's a rehabilitated mass-murderer from Stormcage, the same prison where the 11th Doctor's wife, River Song, served time for killing her husband. He has had neural implants placed inside him to prevent him from being able to kill anybody. He has used his vortex manipulator to travel back to 1955 to prevent the Montgomery bus boycott from occurring, which happens as a result of Rosa Park's being arrested for refusing to give up her seat. The Doctor is determined to keep history in its place, but it won't be easy, for Krasko has already put in place a plan to prevent history from re-occurring, such as having the boss of James Blake giving him the day off, placing false notices at bus stops, vandalizing a bus, and even blocking the route with a car.

Fortunately, Ryan outwits Krasko and uses Krasko's own travel device against him to send him further back in time. When everything has been put back to normal, the Doctor and her friends join the bus route just before Empire theater where Rosa Parks gets on. At that moment, the Doctor realizes they are all playing a part in history and will be forced to witness the pivotal event firsthand. The heart break on Graham's face, when he realizes that he is the white person that Rosa is expected to give up a seat to, is enough to tug at anyone's heartstrings. (This episode was nominated for a BAFTA, but unfortunately did not win). Rosa Parks described herself as being a normal human being like you and I, who was simply tired of giving in.

This is one of the most profound, heart wrenching historical episodes I have ever watched on *Doctor Who*. This episode was extra significant for British viewers as it aired during Black History Month, which falls in October in Britain. The viewing audience will get a unique view of discrimination and segregation African Americans and nonwhite people experienced in the 1950s. Unfortunately, some people still experience racism today simply because they weren't born Caucasian.

I would recommend that viewers have tissues on hand when watching this episode, knowing they are seeing history unfold before their very own eyes.

Episode 4: Arachnids in the UK
Aired: October 28, 2018

Network	BBC One
Writer	Chris Chibnall
Director	Sallie Aprahamian
Producer	Nikki Wilson
Executive Producer(s)	Chris Chibnall, Matt Strevens, Sam Hoyle
Cast	Jodie Whittaker (13th Doctor), Bradley Walsh (Graham O'Brien), Tosin Cole (Ryan Sinclair), Mandip Gill (Yaz)
Guest Cast	Chris Noth (Robertson), Sharon D Clarke (Grace O'Brien), Shobna Gulati (Najia Khan), Tanya Fear (Dr. Jade McIntyre), Ravin J Ganatra (Hakim Khan), Bhavnisha Parmar (Sonya Khan), Jaleh Alp (Frankie Ellish), William Meredith (Kevin)
Rating	8.22m
Fun Fact	Ravin Ganatra, who plays Yaz's Dad, was also briefly in the *Torchwood* episode "Greeks Bearing Gifts."

When the Doctor and her friends arrive back in Sheffield, they quickly realize something has gone very wrong with the spiders that roam the city.

REVIEW

The fourth episode of Series 11, the Doctor has finally gotten her new friends back to Sheffield, but quickly discovers things are not how they left. This episode is full of overdone, unoriginal, giant crawling bugs—a concept that is frequently found in fantasy and young adult stories, and will make anybody who has a phobia of spiders leave the room.

In the history of *Doctor Who*, there have been multiple stories involving the Doctor and giant spiders. In fact, it wasn't that long ago that audiences saw one in *Doctor Who*. The 12th Doctor, during Peter Capaldi's era in the episode "Kill the Moon," had an interesting concept; the moon was actually a giant egg. Throughout the episode the viewers are privy to shots of spider-like creatures who spin webs and kill people.

The episode here, however, centers around a character named Robertson who might remind many viewers of a particular political figure. In this episode, Robertson is an egocentric, corrupt, misogynist. that cares absolutely nothing about the environment or the people around him. He owns several large companies and his only concern is how to earn more money. To get the point across, Robertson had previously ordered waste and chemicals, from 'failed' science experiments run by his various companies, to be dumped in a mine. He attempts to hide this illegal dumping by building a luxury hotel over the site. Yaz's Mom is meant to be the manager of this hotel. That is until she encounters Robertson and a couple of his underlings discussing the illegal dumping and the fact that something frightening has arisen from it. Robertson immediately fires her for interrupting them.

The Doctor and her companions first encounter the spiders in the apartment of one of Yaz's neighbors. They see a coworker of the neighbor trying to enter the apartment to determine why she hadn't shown up for work. Inside, the apartment looks as if it has been abandoned for several years as there are cobwebs everywhere. They find the ill-fated woman in her bed cocooned in spider webs. Then they come face to face with a giant creature. The waste chemicals have led to the development of giant spiders that are infesting the entire city of Sheffield.

Overall the episode was poorly executed and otherwise forgetful. Whether or not Robertson's character is based off an actual person, it would have been more effective in this storytelling had they modeled his character off of the CEO of a large paint manufacturer, whose company was responsible for dumping chemicals into the Flint river in Flint Michigan, which many years later, led to the infamous Flint Water Crisis.

Critics also called this episode boring and recycled. During the Third Doctor's era, there was an episode called "The Green Death," which was literally about a corrupt, corporate executive whose company dumps chemicals into a mine, which resulted in big creepy crawlies. Sound familiar? The coincidences don't stop there. During the 10th Doctor's run, the Doctor also had to confront the Queen of the Eight-Legs in "Planet of the Spiders." The difference was that the Doctor did not go about doing this alone and the spider the 13th Doctor encounters induces much more sympathy from the audience.

There is, however, some additional character development for the companion, Yaz, as the viewing audience gets a glimpse of her family. Her father has a habit of collecting odd things that he finds around town, while her mother has a knack of asking very inappropriate questions of Yaz. For example, she asks Yaz if she and the Doctor were dating. Yaz and the Doctor look at each other and tell her 'NO.' I honestly did not know if she was meaning it as a joke or if the only people Yaz ever brings to her house are people she's dating. And let's not forget her younger sister. She cannot wait for Yaz to move out so she can take over her room. The sibling rivalry is very apparent between Yaz and her sister.

I did not care for this episode at all the first time around, and in my second viewing I fell asleep watching it, therefore, my opinion has not changed. If there was any episode I would even think about suggesting skipping during the 13th Doctor's era, it would be this one.

Episode 5: The Tsuranga Conundrum
Aired: November 4, 2018

Network	BBC One
Writer	Chris Chibnall
Director	Jennifer Perrott
Producer	Nikki Wilson
Executive Producer(s)	Chris Chibnall, Matt Strevens, Sam Hoyle
Cast	Jodie Whittaker (13th Doctor), Bradley Walsh (Graham O'Brien), Tosin Cole (Ryan Sinclair), Mandip Gill (Yaz)
Guest Cast	Brett Goldstein (Astos), Lois Chimimba (Mabi), Suzanne Parker (Eve Cicero), Ben Bailey-Smith (Durkas Cicero), David Shields (Ronan) Jack Shallo (Yoss)
Rating	7.76m
Fun Fact	Pting was created and named by writer, Tim Price

While scavenging on an alien junkyard looking for something for the TARDIS, the Doctor and her friends accidentally get caught in the path of a sonic mine detonation. They wake up aboard a medical space-station where their injuries are being tended to, only to encounter a creature that could be deadlier than the sonic mine detonation.

REVIEW

The fifth episode of Series 11 starts off with an idea that I wish would have been expanded on where the Doctor and her friends are critically injured after getting caught in the path of a sonic mine detonation. They wake up, looking completely fine, aboard some kind of medical space-station, which is on route to a place where their injuries can be further tended to.

The Doctor wants nothing to do with being examined, immediately jumps off the examination table, and starts looking for an exit. This leads to a semi comical foot chase as the two medical technicians chase the Doctor and her companions from room to room trying to stop them from escaping. The Doctor and her companions become separated and she eventually ends up in the main control room and finally realizes that they are indeed on board a ship and getting back to the TARDIS isn't going to be so easy.

It bothered me that no one showed any outward signs of injury, other than the Doctor who is obviously still in quite a bit of pain, till my spouse educated me on concussion grenades used by the military. These grenades, when detonated, do not produce shrapnel. They only produce pressure that causes internal injuries, so, most times the only outward sign of injury seen after one of these devices are used may be bleeding from the mouth, nose, or ears. I believe this to be what the writers had in mind when creating the Sonic Mine.

Still, I feel this may have been a better episode if the writers had shown some type of physical injury, because it would have shown the Doctor being more human-like and permitted the viewing audience to be more sympathetic. Even if the characters showed cuts and/or bruising it would have been better than what we were presented with. I mean, even Superman isn't invincible. While the Sonic Mine may not have produced any shrapnel in and of itself, there were plenty of metal objects in the area that I am sure would have been tossed around in the explosion.

Instead, this episode goes down a road *Doctor Who* has gone down before, creating an environment where the people aboard this space-station become fearful of an unknown enemy and the Doctor must find a way to save them.

The enemy this time is the Pting, an extra-terrestrial that looks like something from the universe of Disney's *Lilo and Stitch*. This creature looks like Stitch's evil cousin from the once dark attraction found at Magic Kingdom's Tomorrowland, "ExtraTERRORestrial Alien Encounter/Stitch's Great Escape." It's a vicious, non-carnivorous bipedal creature, interested in eating inorganic materials, in order to derive energy from them. By the description, it sounds terrifying, but really it turns out to be a disappointment. The creature, through its mannerisms, becomes almost cute—somewhat like the Adipose did in the 10th Doctor's run. While this creature seems bent on destroying the ship to get the energy it craves, it inadvertently saves the day in the end.

While trying to stop this creature from eating them all out of 'ship and home,' the Doctor is made aware of another threat to their survival. The people who built the ship also built a self-destruct mechanism into it. The Doctor is told that, to prevent an alien threat from being brought to the home planet, the powers that be are threatening to use this self-destruct device to destroy the ship and all aboard. The Doctor must find a way to eliminate both threats before they reach the 'point of no return' and the ship is destroyed.

The Doctor devises a plan where the Pting will save them from the self-destruct device. She locates the self-destruct device, a bomb, in the center console of the control room and decides to use the energy to lure the Pting to the last working escape hatch. When the Pting sees the bomb, its eyes light up and it immediately eats the bomb. It explodes inside the Ptings' stomach, presumably providing it with many years of nutrients, and The Doctor ejects it back out into space thus eliminating both threats. The Pting floats off with a very satisfied look on its face rubbing its still glowing belly.

The rest of the story seems to be coming out of the pages of some mpreg (male pregnancy) fan fiction story from ff.net, where the viewing audience discovers one of the passengers on board is pregnant... and male. In this alien race both male and female can become pregnant. The males have boys and the females have girls. Another interesting aspect of this race is that fact that the pregnancy only lasts a week! Oh, and the males, obviously, deliver through C-section. Ryan and Graham find themselves unwilling birth partners as this male passenger 'delivers' his baby with the help of the medical technician. One thing of note is that Ryan is able to convince the new father to keep the boy and raise it himself. While the episode has some ridiculous, yet, silly moments of humor, as a whole it is a let-down.

Episode 6: Demons of the Punjab
Aired: November 11, 2018

Network	BBC One
Writer	Vinay Patel
Director	Jamie Childs
Cast	Jodie Whittaker (13th Doctor), Bradley Walsh (Graham O'Brien), Tosin Cole (Ryan Sinclair), Mandip Gill (Yaz)
Guest Cast	Leena Dhingra (Nani Umbreen), Amita Suman (Umbreen), Shane Zaza (Prem), Hamza Jeetooa (Manish), Shaheen Khan (Hasna), Shobna Gulati (Najia), Ravin J Ganatra (Hakim), Bhavnisha Parmar (Sonya), Emma Fielding (Voice of Kisar), Nathalie Cuzner (Performance of Kisar), Isobel Middleton (Voice of Almak), Barbara Fadden (Performance of Almak)
Rating	7.48m
Fun Fact	The elder Nani Umbreen is supposed to be in her 90s, but the actress playing her, Leena Dhingra, is only in her 70s.

During a birthday celebration for Yaz's Nan Umbreen, Yaz receives a broken watch from her grandmother. Wanting to know more about its origin, Yaz convinces the Doctor and her companions to travel to Punjab where the watch was created. Only to their disbelief, the travelers find themselves caught in the events preceding the partition of India.

REVIEW

The sixth episode of Series 11 returns back to what *Doctor Who* is good at doing: taking an historical event and adding its own flare. This time the viewing audience is taken back to August 1947, after Yaz makes a request to the Doctor to travel to the destination of her Nan's broken watch after she receives it on her Nan's birthday as an heirloom.

When they arrive, the Doctor soon realizes they have traveled back in time to when the partition of India was just beginning. If that wasn't shocking enough, the viewing audience also gets to meet Yaz's Nan, a Hindu, when she was young and about to marry someone that is not Yaz's granddad. Stranger still is that he is a Muslim. In their young minds they felt that their union would prove that the two sanctions could live in harmony together. Anyone get the *Romeo and Juliette* vibe here? Yaz is upset about the fact that the man her gran is about to marry is not her granddad and, throughout this episode, the Doctor has to caution Yaz not to do or say anything that could change history as it would wipe out Yaz's existence. The Doctor's inner turmoil becomes evident when she realizes what is about to happen and the fact that it must happen. She cannot do anything to prevent it as it is a fixed point in time.

The Partition of India was a significant part of world history. Yet, growing up in America, this was my first time even hearing about it. This is honestly frightening to me because this specific time period created the hostile environment between Pakistan and India that can still be found today!

The partition of India involved the division of British India into two independent states, Pakistan and India. Much like America's Civil War, the partition pitted neighbor against neighbor and brother against brother. Two particular provinces, Bengal and Punjab, divided its territories based on the majorities of Hindus or Muslims. As a consequence, between 10-12 million people were displaced along religious lines, creating an overwhelming refugee crisis in the newly constituted dominions; there was large-scale violence, with estimates of the loss of life accompanying and following the partition being disputed between several hundred thousand and two million.

When approaching the subject matter, writer Vinay Patel said in an interview with *Doctor Who Magazine:* "I had a set of rules from the start to help guide myself away from any major missteps. The first was that whatever threats we made up nothing was allowed to be worse than the violence already inherent in that moment in history. Next—related to the first— whatever monsters or aliens we created should be reflective of the thematic concerns of the broader human story. Third, the Doctor could not save the day. These felt like important foundations for us to approach this story with dignity, truth and respect."

Approaching the story with dignity, truth and respect, is exactly what Vinay Patel manages to do.

Patel manages to tell the story without showing favoritism for either side. The writer also revealed in his interview with *Doctor Who Magazine* that he pictured his grandmother when he was writing the role of Yaz's Nan, which I find very touching. Also instead of being filmed in India or Pakistan, this episode was actually filmed in Spain.

There is also a new species of aliens the viewing audience gets to meet called the Thijarians', which at first, seem like they are going to be troublesome, but turn out to be completely different, which provides a nice and moving twist. These aliens appear whenever there is a death. The Doctor mistakenly thinks that they are causing the deaths. Once she is able to confront them, face to face, she finds out she is very wrong. The Thijarians are a warrior race and the two seen in this episode are the last remaining survivors. They have given up their past and now stand watch over those who die with no loved ones around; This is so they will not have to face death alone. They are with the groom when he is killed and bear witness to his death.

The episode aired on Remembrance Day in the UK, and Veteran's Day in the US, which is significant considering the topic. Plus, there are several deliberate close-up shots of poppies throughout the episode.

Like the episode "Rosa," I would recommend that viewers, who are extra sensitive, have tissues on hand.

Episode 7: Kerblam!
Aired: November 18, 2018

Network	BBC One
Writer	Pete McTighe
Director	Jennifer Perrott
Cast	Jodie Whittaker (13th Doctor), Bradley Walsh (Graham O'Brien), Tosin Cole (Ryan Sinclair), Mandip Gill (Yaz)
Guest Cast	Julie Hesmondhalgh (Judy Maddox), Lee Mack (Dan Cooper), Callum Dixon (Jarva Slade), Claudia Jessie (Kira Arlo), Leo Flanagan (Charlie Duffy), Matthew Gravelle (Voice of Kerblam)
Rating	7.46m
Fun Fact	Pete McTighe specifically wrote the character of Dan Cooper for comedian, Lee Mack. Pete also writes the booklets found inside the *Doctor Who* Blu-ray box sets

When the Doctor receives a package that a previous incarnation of hers ordered from a delivery company called Kerblam. She is stunned to find a message hidden in the box requesting the Doctor's help. The Doctor and her companions decide to travel to Kerblam to investigate the mysterious message, only to discover more is going on than just meets the eye.

REVIEW

The seventh episode of Series 11 is one of my favorite episodes because it's light-hearted and feels very *Doctor Who-ish*. It's a needed change of pace after the last couple of episodes, plus, I absolutely adore the clever nod to the 11th Doctor by the item that's waiting inside a surprise delivery box for the Doctor.

Jodie Whittaker's Doctor becomes very excited, like a child about to unwrap a Christmas present, when she receives a special gift delivered unexpectedly by a Kerblam! man, who is a robot from the factory Kerblam! She admits that she doesn't recall ordering anything, so it had to be from a while ago. She's right; it turns out to be the replacement fez the 11th Doctor ordered, and… a note that asks for help. Because the Doctor can never turn down a plea for help, she and her friends come up with a plan. They pretend to be new hired workers for Kerblam! With the help of the Doctor's psychic paper and a little sleight of hand with her sonic, they are able to trick the human resources woman and are allowed to enter the factory.

The big question I had throughout this entire episode is: with how efficient and technologically advanced this company has become, why did it take literally two regenerations for the Doctor to receive her order? Was it because the Doctor had to input a specific coordinate and she had not traveled to that location until now? I'm certain the 11th Doctor didn't deliberately schedule to have his replacement fez arrive billions of years late!

#TeamTARDIS arrives at the moon-size warehouse that is orbiting a very distant future Earth. I cannot help but be reminded of those big-box store chains like Walmart/Sam's Club or even a warehouse like Amazon. What is immediately obvious about this place is there are more robot workers dressed as Postmen than human workers. In fact, one of the human workers admits that Kerblam runs on a 10% organic workforce: organic meaning human. And that's kind of what this story is ultimately about, the whole idea of robots replacing human workers, causing people to lose their jobs because of ever evolving technology. When you think about it, that's been going on for a while and as technology progresses, it becomes worse. Nowadays one cannot even go into a McDonald's without being forced to use a germ filled touchscreen to place their orders. Also, let us not forget the unforgivable U-scans, or self-checkouts, that are popping up in just about every store.

But, with any controversial business practices, there are bound to be detractors—groups of people who are not happy with the way the establishment is doing things. Radicals if you will. Kerblam certainly has its fair share of problems with these groups protesting the replacement of human workers by nonhuman, or robot, workers. One example of this is a fun fact I learned from one of the actors who played one of the Kerblam! mans. He stated water was rationed in packets for those who worked in the factory and they were required to keep their Kerblam heads in buckets to prevent them from getting damaged.

But organic workers to nonorganic workers isn't the only thing going on in this episode. Organic workers have suddenly started disappearing and power surges have been plaguing the warehouse, and no one seems to know why. Or at least, no one is talking. It would appear that one of those radical groups have infiltrated the Kerblam! workforce. Someone working behind the scenes is sabotaging the warehouse.

The Doctor and her companions are 'evaluated' to find which job in the warehouse they are best fitted for. Turns out Graham is suited for janitorial work. He befriends a young man, one of the current janitors, and gets him to tell all he knows about the inner workings of Kerblam. Meanwhile the Doctor and Ryan are sent to the 'packing' department to work and Yaz is sent to the warehouse to retrieve items that have been ordered.

As the Doctor is trying to unravel the mystery, she can't help but notice that they are being carefully watched by the robots. She asks one of the other workers in the department how someone would be able to send out a message on a packing slip. The worker says that would be impossible as the packing slips are produced and packed by machine. This perplexes the Doctor and the mystery deepens.

The Doctor decided that a direct approach is needed and confronts the CEO of Kerblam! and the head of human resources. The CEO denies that anything is amiss at first but then confesses that he has been trying to figure out the disappearance of his employees. The head of human resources is completely flabbergasted because according to her computers no one is missing. Every single organic being is accounted for. Graham and his new friend arrive followed closely by a Kerblam! man. This robot attacks Graham's friend and the robot is immediately beheaded by the head of human resources.

The Doctor uses this head to search the Kerblam computers and discovers that it was the original computer droid that sent the 'HELP' message. It had detected a problem among the robot workforce and needed help to stop it. Using the original droid, the doctor is able to figure out the plot. It seems that Graham's new friend was a plant by a rebel group that was plotting to destroy Kerblam by sending out Kerblam! men carrying bombs. But these bombs aren't your typical bombs. They are bubble wrap filled with an explosive gas. When you pop the bubbles... BOOM! The Doctor is able to foil the evil plot by having the original droid reprogram the Kerblam! men to deliver their packages to themselves, open the packages, and pop the bubble wrap blowing themselves up.

I can guarantee by the end of the episode, you'll never look at bubble wrap the same ever again. This episode is fun, light-hearted, asks the big question whether we want to be replaced by technology, while executing this *Doctor Who* episode at its best.

Episode 8: The Witchfinders

Aired: November 25, 2018

Network	BBC One
Writer	Joy Wilkinson
Director	Sallie Aprahamian
Cast	Jodie Whittaker (13th Doctor), Bradley Walsh (Graham O'Brien), Tosin Cole (Ryan Sinclair), Mandip Gill (Yaz)
Guest Cast	Alan Cumming (King James), Siobhan Finneran (Becka Savage), Tilly Steele (Willa Twiston), Tricia Kelly (Old Mother Twiston), Arthur Kay (Smithy), Stavros Demetraki (Alfonso)
Rating	7.21m
Fun Fact	The old Pendle Witches walking trail refers to the Lancashire Witches Walk, which opened in 2012 to commemorate the 400th anniversary of the Pendle Witch Trials

The Doctor and her companions travel to 17th century Lancashire only to find themselves caught up in a witch hunt held by a local landowner.

REVIEW

The eighth episode of *Doctor Who* has an ironic story behind its original airdate. While the viewing audience was able to enjoy the previous episode that eerily could have been compared to Amazon, fans in the US who happened to have the streaming service Amazon Prime, had a totally different surprise. This episode was accidentally leaked an entire week early! Or was it accidental? Was Amazon trying to distract us from the underlying subject of the previous episode? We will probably never know whether that truly was an innocent error or if that was Amazon's way of saying they were "watching."

Nonetheless, this is an episode of *Doctor Who* that can make the viewing audience feel both uncomfortable and frightened at the same time. When the Doctor and her friends travel to 17th century Lancashire they find themselves in what appears to be England's own version of the Salem Witch Trials. On the day they arrive there is to be a 'trial' of a 'witch.' The people of the village have taken to making it a festive affair, as it seems to happen every weekend, by gathering in the town square having cookouts and bobbing for apples. The Doctor exclaims, "I love bobbing for apples!" and goes in for one. Just as she emerges a bell is rung, and all the people head for the pond. There a woman has been tied to a large tree branch and is about to be dunked in the water to see if she is indeed a 'witch.' If she survives, she is a witch and will be burned at the stake. If she drowns then she would be deemed to be innocent. Some justice there. NOT! The Doctor decides to put a stop to these 'trials.'

I'll admit I absolutely hated this episode during my first viewing. Growing up I was pretty fascinated by the Salem Witch trials, so for me, my mind immediately concluded that episode was more about politics where people were just naming people, instead of it being really about Becka Savage keeping her secret, therefore, I had felt it poorly executed.

That's not the first time I've completely missed the ball. It's hard for me to forget that the first time around watching Matt Smith's incarnation of the 11th Doctor, I couldn't stand Matt because I had such a difficult time wrapping my head around how the Doctor with so much emotional baggage could suddenly become so silly. I felt like it was as if the actor himself was mocking the whole character! But that wasn't what Matt was doing at all (and I feel terribly embarrassed to admit I even thought that to begin with! In case Matt may be reading this, I'm so sorry. I am an idiot.)

This is the first time where the viewing audience gets to see the Doctor struggle getting her message across now that she's female, and because of that, she is challenged like she has never been challenged before. She's able to convince the magistrate that she is the Witch Finder General and calls a stop to the trials until she can investigate. Just when it seems like the Doctor is making some progress, King James I, played by Alan Cumming who had been wanting to play a part in the show for a while, arrives and instantly assumes that Graham is the one in charge. He scoffs at the idea that the Doctor is the one in charge because she is, of course, female. It becomes evident that during that time in history women were thought of as lesser beings than men and therefore could not hold a role of authority over men. Unless they were royalty of course.

The evil shows up in the form of reanimated corpses. These corpses, now engulfed in mud, were once innocent people, slaughtered to keep something secret, unlike the true witch hunts of that period in time. There is a twist to this story however that is surprising. While the corpses seem to be bent on destroying a certain person, we find this is not the case at all and a new alien race is introduced to the watching audience.

It is discovered that the magistrate has been possessed by the alien race that had been imprisoned on the planet Earth in its very early days. The magistrate had been using the witch trials to gather an army who would also by possessed by the aliens. The reanimated corpses were coming to her aid, not to destroy her. The Doctor is able to re-incarcerate the aliens and free the dead so they can now rest in peace.

The cinematography is stunning as a close-up of these corpses are nothing like the walkers from *The Walking Dead*, but more like something that should come out of some Asian Horror flick or even *the Ring*. These corpses are fully formed, not rotting like the typical 'zombie.'

This episode is a story within a political story and if the viewing audience misses that, like I did the first time through, you'll come out of this episode with a complete misunderstanding. Be cautious, there's more going on than meets the eye.

I would also caution viewers with young children. While *Doctor Who* is supposed to be a children's show, this episode is not one of those, and could leave a young child with nightmares.

Episode 9: It Takes You Away

Aired: December 2, 2018

Network	BBC One
Writer	Ed Hime
Director	Jamie Childs
Cast	Jodie Whittaker (13th Doctor), Bradley Walsh (Graham O'Brien), Tosin Cole (Ryan Sinclair), Mandip Gill (Yaz)
Guest Cast	Sharon D Clarke (Grace), Eleanor Wallwork (Hanne), Kevin Eldon (Ribbons), Christian Rubeck (Erik), Lisa Stokke (Trine)
Rating	6.42m
Fun Fact	While this episode's story is supposed to be taking place in Norway, it was actually filmed in south Wales

The Doctor and her companions travel to Norway where they investigate the disappearance of a widower named Erik.

REVIEW

The ninth episode of Series 11 is my favorite episode of the series. It has everything a *Doctor Who* episode should have—mystery, suspense, odd things, magic mirrors, alternative dimensions, and, oh, did I mention a frog that can talk?

This episode we can also see the how much Jodie Whittaker has grown into her role, though her Doctor still needs some significant character development. She no longer has a bunch of clever one liners and now is more comfortable, confident, and can speak a mile a minute.

The TARDIS travels to Norway, where they meet a young girl, Hanne, who is alone, blind, and scared in a cabin in the woods. Upon entering the cabin, they discover that there is very little food to be found. Concerned for this girl they question her about her circumstances. The Doctor and her friends learn that Hanne's father has gone missing and there's some kind of growling monster in the woods.

"My character is blind," Ellie Wallwork explained in an interview with *Doctor Who Magazine*. Ellie Wallwork, the actress portraying Hanne, is actually blind, which makes her characterization that much more realistic to the viewing audience because she is able to provide an interpretation a sighted actor or actress could not. And while the actress is British, she can pull off a Norwegian accent with no difficulties. "Hanne has been left alone for four days before the Doctor and her friends come. She doesn't have any means to prepare food, really, so, she's starving and there are these monsters in the woods. She's terrified and is feeling really horrible."

The Doctor and the companions learn that Hanne's mother died, so it is just her and her father. Her father has gone missing before, usually for two or three days, but would later reappear with food and such for Hanne before disappearing again. He explains his disappearances as 'hunting trips' or 'trips into town.' They live on a small island so the only way into town is by boat. She tells the companions not to worry because she knows her father would not totally abandon her with a monster in the woods. When questioned about the monster, Hanne can only say that it appears at a certain time of the day and her father has cautioned her to not go near the windows or be outdoors when this time comes. Hanne says she can feel when the monster is about to appear and that she has only ever heard its cry.

The Doctor sends Yaz and Ryan out to investigate the surrounding area while she and Graham search the cabin for clues. Ryan and Yaz enter a shed on the property and find several animal carcasses that have been hung from the rafters with ropes, presumably to age for meat. They also discover something that seems quite strange, a set of speakers connected to a tape player. Ryan and Yaz return to the cabin to find Hanne upset and the Doctor trying to calm her down. Hanne says that the monster is about to appear, and she needs to find a place to hide. The next moment the most horrific screeching and moaning sound is heard. Hanne crouches down and covers her ears. Ryan and Yaz are looking through holes in the boards covering the windows trying to get a glimpse of the monster but see nothing.

Graham is still searching the cabin and enters the master bedroom on the upper floor. In this room he sees a mirror on the far wall. The mirror appears strange somehow, but Graham can't quite figure it out. The glass almost appears to be liquid instead of solid. Then he hears the monster outside. He looks out a window but sees nothing. It is at this point that the noise stops. Graham calls down to the Doctor which brings everyone upstairs into the room. The Doctor agrees that the mirror isn't right. It appears to be a portal of some type.

While it appears, this episode will be about the Doctor and her friends figuring out the identification of the monster, and how to get rid of it, the viewing audience is instead treated to inter-dimensional travel, where they not only locate Hanne's father and, what appears to be her mother, but also someone else completely unexpected. Grace appears to Graham. While he is understandably upset and willing to give in to the deception, he knows it is a trick and his heart breaks again as he must leave 'Grace' behind once more.

Inter-dimensional travel is not unheard of in the *Doctor Who* universe. Older viewers of *Doctor Who* will recall the 10th Doctor had to leave behind one of his beloved companions, Rose, in an alternative version of Earth, after she had been exposed to traveling between inter-dimensional worlds too much and she could no longer survive in the Doctor's world.

In this episode, the Doctor must confront the Solitract. These creatures capture and take over the lives of their victims by appearing as a loved one that has passed on. They create new lives for these people and live through them. They appear to the Doctor, singularly, as a talking frog. The Doctor is able to convince the Solitract to let the others go by offering herself and her many hundreds of years and adventures as a sacrifice. By doing so the Doctor knows she is putting herself in grave danger. It is interesting how she is able to talk the Solitract into letting her go as well.

Ultimately, this episode's subject matter is death, but it is handled in a way that leaves the viewing audience feeling uplifted.

Episode 10: The Battle of Ranskoor Av Kolos

Aired: December 9, 2018

Network	BBC One
Writer	Chris Chibnall
Director	Jamie Childs
Cast	Jodie Whittaker (13th Doctor), Bradley Walsh (Graham O'Brien), Tosin Cole (Ryan Sinclair), Mandip Gill (Yaz)
Guest Cast	Phyllis Logan (Andinio), Mark Addy (Paltraki), Percelle Ascott (Delph), Samuel Oatley (Tzim-Sha), Jan Le (Umsang)
Rating	6.65m
Fun Fact	The Doctor makes a reference to accomplishments made by her Ninth and Tenth incarnations

The Doctor and her companions travel to the planet Ranskoor Av Kolos and come across an old foe. Tzim-Sha is attempting to use the psychic powers of the Ux race in order to shrink the Earth and take revenge for his exile and defeat.

REVIEW

The final episode of Series 11 is the one that really pulls this entire series together. While the viewing audience learns of a new species of people called the Ux who are capable of doing things simply by thought, they also discover an old foe has returned, desperate to find some inferior species he can use to plot his revenge.

The Ux have created a large Citadel that they live in and are helping the Doctor's old foe who they mistakenly think is their god. They unwittingly help this 'god' in his evil plot to get back at the Doctor. This is an episode where the viewing audience starts to get a clearer picture of the Stenza's true nature. Yes, there was "the Ghost Monument" episode where we were able to see an environment after genocide has occurred, but not while the destruction was still occurring.

When the Doctor and her friends arrive to investigate the source of a distress signal, they find a world that looks like it was most recently a battleground. Debris is everywhere and there doesn't appear to be any survivors. They enter one of the downed space crafts and start to investigate, trying to figure out what happened. It is here that they come upon Paltraki, played by Mark Addy, whose mission is hidden inside his muddled brain. (For anyone reading this who may be also a fan of the *Game of Thrones* television series, Mark Addy also played the role of Robert Baratheon). Since Paltraki's initial arrival, the planet has been attacking his brain, so it's all confused and jumbled. When the Doctor tries to ask him about what happened, he cannot even remember his own name let alone have a conversation for more than a minute. He even seems to forget that he had been talking with the Doctor as he raises his weapon and asks again who she is and how she got there.

The Doctor offers Paltraki a device that would prevent the planet from further attacking his brain and help him straighten out his thoughts. He soon remembers who he is and what his mission was. He was originally sent to capture these crystal shards but cannot yet remember what is inside them or why he has to retrieve them. He reveals that many have tried before him and have failed. Those are the other destroyed space craft seen littered around the area.

Their discussion is cut off by a transmission from an unknown source demanding that Paltraki return what he has taken, or his crew will be killed. It is during this transmission that the Doctor and her companions hear a familiar voice. The Doctor and her friends discover the real horror: Tim Shaw arrived on this planet after he was zapped out of Sheffield and has since become much more powerful. He blames the Doctor for his current state and expresses his need for revenge.

This is the first time where I really noticed the difference between Jodie's Doctor and previous incarnations when she was faced with Tim Shaw's plan. He is using the Ux to carry out his revenge on the Doctor by taking planets hostage, imprisoning them in the crystal shards, and destroying the people living on them. And Earth is his next target. You can see the conflict in the Doctor's face when she demands Tim Shaw not to blame what happened to him on her. While effective, she was honestly pretty calm compared to how Matt Smith or Peter Capaldi's Doctors would have reacted.

This episode also helps to close an important story arc for Graham and Ryan as they confront their feelings of seeing Tim Shaw back after losing Grace. Graham took the Doctor aside and told her that if he sees this monster, he will not hesitate to kill him. The Doctor tells Graham to return to the TARDIS, but he refuses and follows the Doctor to the Citadel where Tim Shaw and the Ux are holed up. When confronted by the possibility of having to face Tim Shaw, Ryan is able to talk Graham into being the 'bigger, better man.' In the end Graham does end up shooting Tim Shaw but he does not kill the creature. It's an episode that will keep you feeling on the edge of your seat until the very end.

Something tells me we haven't seen the last of Tim Shaw or the Stenza yet.

New Year's Special: Resolution
Aired: January 1, 2019

Network	BBC One
Writer	Chris Chibnall
Director	Wayne Yip
Cast	Jodie Whittaker (13th Doctor), Bradley Walsh (Graham O'Brien), Tosin Cole (Ryan Sinclair), Mandip Gill (Yaz)
Guest Cast	Charlotte Ritchie (Lin), Nikesh Patel (Mitch), Daniel Adegboyega (Aaron), Darryl Clark (Police Office Will), Connor Calland (Security Guard Richard), James Lewis (Farmer Dinkle), Sophie Duval (Mum), Callum McDonald (Teen 1), Harry Vallance (Teen 2), Laura Evelyn (Call Centre Polly), Michael Ballard (Sergeant), Nick Briggs (Voice of the Dalek)
Rating	7.3m
Fun Fact	Yaz was originally supposed to be controlled by the Dalek mutant. This was changed due to time restraints. This is also the only *Doctor Who* episode to air in 2019.

On this New Year's Day 2019 Special, the 13th Doctor first encounters a new design of the Daleks with new weaponry, which includes possession and multiple short-range missiles behind its orbs. Ryan's character arc is further expanded by the introduction of his father, and the conflict Ryan has referred to previously in the series.

REVIEW

Christmas has been a tradition for *Doctor Who* fans of getting to spend part of theirs with the Doctor since the show's revival, but last year, that tradition was broken. Instead, the viewing audience got to spend part of their New Year's Day. While fans were gracious to have the Doctor on their TVs, some expressed dissatisfaction for Chibnall for purposefully breaking tradition. However, those who tuned in got to see the return of the Doctor's greatest enemy, the Dalek, with an upgraded design, making it now capable of controlling another person's will.

This episode begins with a big ancient battle where the people appear to be battling a common foe. This foe is defeated, and its carcass divided into three parts. It is decided that these parts will be dispersed to the farthest reaches of the planet and will be watched over throughout eternity. However, one of the carriers is ambushed and killed, and that particular part is lost to history.

Fast forward to present times and an archaeological dig. The Archaeologists uncover this thing that they can't quite identify. They set it aside for later inspection. One of the archaeologists spills something on the equipment and the specimen causing it to reanimate. Neither of them notices this and close down for the night. The next day they discover that the specimen is missing.

The archaeologists decide to continue with their investigating of the dig site, and one goes off to explore. She soon finds what looks like an octopus climbing up one of the walls (any long-time fan of the show knows exactly what this creature is). She is excited by her find and immediately runs to grab her partner. She is stopped cold when she notices the Doctor and her Companions wandering in the tunnel as there is not supposed to be anyone else there. She is joined by her partner and she tells him what she has found. The Doctor gets a little chill up her spine and asks her to take them to where this thing was. When they get back the creature is gone. Only a faint outline remains of what the creature looked like.

Despite showrunner Chris Chibnall stating Jodie's first series would not contain any old monsters, it is possible he wasn't referencing this episode since he was planning on it airing in the following year. But even with an old monster, Chibnall successfully was able to make it "new." For example, this Dalek was split into three parts outside of its normal makeshift casing. Once a part of it was reanimated it was able to reconnect with the remaining two parts. Also, in the first time in the show's history, this Dalek was not controlled by an actor from the inside, and instead, was done by remote control.

Once this Dalek was reconnected to all its parts, it set about building a new outer shell. Being close to the Iron Works in Sheffield it had plenty of material to work with. It also had a new armor that could easily make it capable of taking out an entire army by itself.

Its weapons have been upgraded as well. It now has guided missiles behind its skirt domes.

The viewing audience also got to see the Doctor model off a new scarf. This new scarf got quite the attention when it debuted in online stores. The first time I saw it, it reminded me of the gigantic scarf the Fourth Doctor used to wear, except it appears to be made out of linen with rainbow colors. It would appear other fans felt the same way because once a version of it ended up online, it sold like hotcakes and was quickly sold out.

However, what most fans don't know is that scarf was added to the Doctor's costume by accident. It was actually a gift for the production designer, Arwel Wyn Jones, from his wife Claire Pritchard, who also worked on the set as the make-up designer. Chris Chibnall revealed in an interview: "Arwel wore it around the production. Ray Holman, the costume designer, saw it and thought it would be perfect for Jodie's Doctor. Ray showed it to Jodie, who loved it, and he saved it for the Special."

There is also a wardrobe malfunction that takes place with Jodie's stunt double, which is the Easter egg for this episode. After the Dalek states 'the Doctor is an enemy of all Dalek,' the audience sees the Doctor jump and flip out of the way of the Dalek's extermination shots. However, if you slow down the scene just after she starts flipping, her stunt double's wig falls off, revealing it's not really Jodie performing at that time.

This episode also wraps up the character arc of Ryan Sinclair when his deadbeat father finally shows himself, making for some awkward moments. Graham takes Ryan's father aside and makes sure that he will not hurt Ryan as he has done in the past. Ryan's father explains that he isn't there to cause trouble. He is just trying to get a new venture off the ground. He is now selling microwave ovens door to door. Ryan is extremely cautious but agrees to go to dinner with his father where he finds out about his fathers' current line of work. Ryan, having none of the nonsense, tells his father exactly how he feels and that he could care less if his father were to disappear again.

The Doctor, having confronted the new Dalek, learns of its mission and tracks it to the military base from which the nuclear missiles are launched. She tries to contact UNIT (Unified Intelligence Taskforce) only to discover that UNIT has been dissolved due to some political rivalries among international partners. Ryan's father joins the crew as he wants to help rid the world of this threat. It turns out that this is a fortuitous event as it is Ryan's father who ends up saving the day with his microwave knowledge. And Ryan learns that he still loves his father despite all that has happened in the past.

Overall, while not the best episode I've seen for *Doctor Who*, it did make me wish that there wasn't going to be this long year wait. Until next time!

If You Only Watch One Episode

"Bit of adrenaline, dash of outrage and a hint of panic knitted my brain back together. I know exactly who I am. I'm the Doctor. Sorting out fair play throughout the universe."
- 13th Doctor

If you only had the opportunity to watch one episode from Series 11, the question would be, which episode represents the best reflection of the Doctor's character? For me, that is *The Ghost Monument*, which is the second installment in this series. In this episode fans of the show previously will recognize this being a key moment when the Doctor really comes into herself.

Discussed in an earlier chapter of this book, I mentioned briefly how the Doctor has never been a fan of weapons. She prefers having to be forced to use the skills of her brain, keeping her on her toes, and outwitting her enemy. Perhaps, she simply loves the challenge!

This episode we also get to see her compassion for the past residents of Desolation, a society that became lost due to the Stenza forcing them to create weapons of mass destruction, ultimately forcing their own genocide. Again, viewers of *Doctor Who* could believe she may be thinking about her own people who were lost during the Time War.

The audience also gets to see a brief moment where the Doctor shows human like qualities of inner struggle when she encounters the cloth-like creatures called the Remnants, who mention she is afraid of being forgotten, unloved and unwanted. Even though she is an alien with two hearts, it is in this particular moment, when she appears most vulnerable and human.

After You've Watched

"... 'cause we're all capable of the most incredible change. We can evolve while still staying true to who we are. We can honor who we've been and choose who we want to be next."
-13th Doctor

"I do not believe *Doctor Who* was preaching," Tosin Cole, who played Ryan Sinclair, said in an interview when discussing the Rosa Parks episode in Series 11. "I think it was reigniting the fire, like these issues are still going on today, it's going on now. Let's be aware of what's going on. *Doctor Who* should be educating and inspiring a younger audience. It is reflecting historical and contemporary society and sparking conversations about race and equality. It's current. It's one of the most current things going on today. Those issues are still going on now. That's why it was so refreshing to see that. Seeing someone who was having a struggle years ago, and to still see that struggle today in a way, it hits home."

Doctor Who serves us, the audience, as our guide, our *Sherpa*. Just as we're following the Doctor and the various companions through their personal journeys, we're also making that same journey through life, as we seek answers to life's most important questions—who we are, why we're here and where we're going. Since 1963, the Doctor's and the companions' stories have connected thousands of television fans on a human level, and Chibnall has continued this tradition in Series 11 by integrating real historical stories, while delivering its message that we're all connected and should be included. People's existence is not politics; they're facts.

Series 12 will continue this theme in addition to introducing a new theme—identity. The companions this time will travel with the Doctor because they want to, not because of some happy accident, like what occurred in *The Woman Who Fell to Earth*. Not only will they learn to discover they need the Doctor, but the Doctor will come to realize she also needs them. They will continue their personal growth journeys together while they seek out the answers to the questions we must all face.

However, I believe this theme has already begun to be established. Throughout this series, the audience got to see Graham and Ryan grow, Yaz learned how to be stronger and more confident, and the Doctor got to continue doing what she has always been good at, protecting the universe.

Let's take a deeper look into the stories of Graham, Ryan and Yaz and see how it all comes together.

Graham

In *The Woman Who Fell to Earth* we first meet Graham on top of Garth Mountain alongside his wife, Grace, where they are trying their best to encourage their grandson, Ryan, to ride a bicycle. Graham is a handsome, charming, witty, older gentleman with a caring nature. The audience learns he is a former bus driver and really enjoyed that job until he was no longer able to perform the job's duties.

The family dynamics are interesting because Graham's notably the only Caucasian, and the audience can sense right away that the step-granddad/step-grandson relationship isn't perfect simply because Ryan refuses to address his step-granddad by any other name than Graham. Grace is outgoing and more adventurous, willing to take risks, while Graham tends to stay more in her shadow, questioning everything before jumping right into it.

Graham clearly has an inner struggle going on. He is torn whether he is good enough to be a proper granddad for Ryan. Though he never indicates it, he may have even been questioning his relationship with Grace, simply because if he's not good enough for her grandson, how can he expect that he can continue to be good enough for her? Sure, he moved from Essex to Sheffield to live with her, and he has his life literally to thank her for, but who's to say he didn't experience the nightingale effect?

Before this conflict can be resolved, the Doctor literally crash lands into the train he and Grace are traveling on. He soon discovers he has no choice but help the Doctor and his friends any way he can, including retrieving information from other bus drivers.

The relationship struggle between Ryan and Graham becomes even more obvious after Ryan admits to the Doctor that he may be the one responsible for bringing the alien and its spaceship to Earth. Graham is frustrated and accuses Ryan of using his disability as an excuse while Grace tries to get him to calm down and be fair.

Just when Graham is starting to feel sure of himself, his world is turned upside down as Grace unexpectedly dies during an encounter with aliens. He almost immediately begins to experience survivor's guilt. It's clear to him that he should have been the one who died and not her. After all, he had been dying from cancer not too long ago and Grace had, in fact, been his caretaker. He has no idea how to raise Ryan properly without her and clearly wanted more time with Grace.

In *The Ghost Monument*, Graham continues this inner struggle as well as his relationship with Ryan. He watches Ryan continue to distance himself and get angry any time Grace's name is brought up. Graham feels helpless, not knowing what the best thing to do or say is until he finally has the guts to confront Ryan about not opening up about his feeling about Grace's death.

By the episode *Rosa*, Graham is gaining more confidence and courage to stand up for his friends and beliefs. There are multiple times when he could have failed to acknowledge to the racist people living in Montgomery, Alabama, that he was Ryan's step-granddad. Instead, he continued to proudly do so. He tells the gang that the first time he met Grace she informed him, after learning that he was a bus driver, that he better be not like that James Blake guy (the bus driver who was driving the bus the night Rosa Parks refused to give up her seat). However, there is still one thing that's quite clear about his character in this episode, and that's he's a white man experiencing America's white privileges no matter how good a person he may be trying to be.

Ultimately, Graham gets to deliver one of the most significant lines that drove both his role and the Doctor's this series—"I don't want to be part of this." He's definitely uncomfortable when they are forced to stay on the bus in order to play their part in history and allow Rosa Parks the opportunity to refuse to give up her seat, not because of her situation, but instead, because he has allowed injustice to go on in silence, which if you think about it, still often occurs today. For example, how many times have you heard about a woman or man getting beaten up or shot on the street, and people simply walk on?

In *Arachnid in the UK*, Graham goes home for the first time since losing Grace. It is in this episode, where he comes to the realization that he isn't ready to go back to a life without her at his side, and he'd rather travel with the Doctor. "The thing about grief is that it needs time."

It isn't until episode nine, *It Takes You Away*, where we finally get movement in Graham and Ryan's storyline and their grieving process. This episode provides an important lesson that while moving on is necessary, it isn't something that happens overnight. In fact, it's easier said than done. Here, Ryan is the one who comes to the conclusion that they have each other and finally starts to call Graham his granddad.

In *The Battle of Ranskoor Av Kolos*, Graham is tested like never before and brings out a side of him after all his character development that I didn't think was possible. When the Doctor and her friends end up on a dangerous planet where someone is trying to collect vibrating boxes, they quickly realize the alien responsible for Grace's death, Tzim-Sha, has become even deadlier. Graham vows to kill Tzim-Sha and avenge the death of his wife, which is something the Doctor cannot allow, even if Tzim-Sha may deserve it. Ultimately, when Graham comes face-to-face with Tzim-Sha, with a gun in his hand, he is unable to commit murder, not because he doesn't want to, but simply because he knows in his heart that he's a better man and that Grace wouldn't want it.

Series 11 concludes with a special New Year's episode titled *Resolution*, which serves as a powerful episode for Graham when Ryan's estranged father, Aaron, finally decides to show up. While the Doctor and everyone else is off fighting the Dalek, Graham and Aaron are left behind so they can sort things out. Graham presents Aaron with a box of Grace's things to demonstrate how much he missed in both her life and his son's by not being there. It is this action, which ultimately helps Aaron regret his wrongdoings and re-create the bond between the three of them after Ryan saves his father from the Dalek.

Ryan

We first meet Ryan in *The Woman Who Fell to Earth* as a 19-year-old man, on top of Garth Mountain. To merely say he's having a bad day is an understatement. Ryan suffers from dyspraxia, which means he has trouble with coordination and, therefore, has been unable to learn how to ride a bicycle. He has been trying his best to learn, because he wanted to make his Nan (Grace) proud. While Grace assures him that she is proud of him, he cannot believe it, as he continues to fall over and over again. He becomes so disgusted with himself that he ends up throwing his bike down the mountain, to both Grace and Graham's horror!

This is not the only turmoil Ryan is dealing with. His Nan has married a new man, who is trying to call him son, but he wants none of it. Right now, he cannot see Graham as any thing other than his Nan's husband. This is partially due to his mother suddenly passing years earlier, and his father abandoning him after she died. Perhaps, he is afraid the same thing will happen to Graham, too, if he attempts to get close. So, instead, he acts defensive and dismissive.

Ryan's inner turmoil becomes more obvious when in the warehouse in front of the Doctor, Grace and Yaz, Graham abruptly accuses him of using his disability as an excuse for allowing an alien to come to planet Earth, when he touched something floating in the air while he was attempting to retrieve his bike. Yaz decides to take Ryan aside, and that's when he admits to her that Graham simply doesn't understand him. Later, Ryan does ultimately get to assist the Doctor with Tzim-Sha by climbing up a ladder to reach a crane, from which he almost slips and falls to his death, but fortunately manages to get the task done.

It would appear Graham was not the only one who doesn't understand Ryan. When his Nan is suddenly killed by Tzim-Sha, his father promises to be there for his Nan's funeral. However, he lets Ryan and the rest of the family down, never showing up, thus, leaving Ryan feeling he isn't important or worthy of his father's love.

In *The Ghost Monument*, Ryan is still working on his relationship with Graham. After attempting to get an old boat started for the Doctor and the rest of the gang, he ends up being forced to have a heart-to-heart conversation regarding his Nan's death as Graham is also still learning to cope. Ryan's coping mechanism dealing with his Nan's passing is simply to not discuss it at all, which Graham doesn't approve of.

Shortly afterward, he attempts to show how cool he is with a weapon by running out in the open and shooting the robot snipers that are after him and his friends, unaware it will only temporarily deactivate them. The Doctor is not impressed and has an argument with him, eventually one upping him to prove her point of not needing weapons and only needing to use one's brain. The audience can further sense Ryan's frustration when he's forced to have to climb down another ladder and at a quicker speed than usual. "Ladders. Why does it always have to be ladders?"

In the episode, *Rosa,* the audience gets to learn a bit more about Ryan's upbringing after he is abruptly slapped in the face for assisting a white woman who dropped an item in then-segregated Montgomery, Alabama. He explains his Nan raised him to control his temper, even though he really wanted to sock the man who slapped him. This is the first episode where Ryan both shines and shows a sense of hopelessness. He temporarily forgets why the civil rights movement was so important in America's history. All he can really concentrate on is how presently he is being made to feel he is unwelcome simply because of the color of his skin. He forgets the civil rights movement helped end segregation and creates opportunities and hope for people like him and future generations, including making the way for the first African

American President. Perhaps, it was his conversation with Yaz, and spending time with Rosa Parks and Martin Luther King Jr., that gave him the courage to finally stand up to the racist, Krasko.

In *Arachnid in the UK*, Ryan receives a letter from his father, which makes him start to realize that not only is his father family, but so is Graham, too.

In *The Tsuranga Conundrum*, Ryan realizes he can trust Yaz and opens up to her about his mother and Nan's passing. We also get to understand Ryan still carries a lot of pain inside him from his father abandoning him. When the character, Yoss, expresses his fears about fatherhood, Ryan helps Yoss believe in himself again and that he is more than cut out for fatherhood. In fact, he is going to be an excellent father. At this moment, Ryan expresses everything that he wished his father could have been for him.

By the time we reach the episode *It Takes You Away,* we see Ryan tentatively reach out to Graham and call him Grandad for the first time. We can see Ryan has grown just a little emotionally as he realizes that Graham may be all he has in life. Graham is willing to accept this baby step and continues to encourage Ryan in little ways such as continually reaching out for that fist bump.

Yaz

In *The Woman Who Fell to Earth* we first meet Yaz as a patrol officer in training when she is faced with sorting out an incident between two women having a go at each other over a car accident. Yaz, while she enjoys her job, has been becoming bored with it. She's frustrated. She doesn't feel she's being challenged enough, nor does she feel she is being used to the best of her abilities. She wants something more, and the universe happily grants her that wish when Ryan abruptly calls the police to report an unidentified object.

When Yaz arrives at the scene, she honestly thinks Ryan is pulling a prank. That is, until she realizes that Ryan is the same Ryan Sinclair she attended school with. However, her day will only get a lot stranger. Ryan receives a call from his Nan that something has happened with the train she and Graham are on, and Yaz decides to take action. It is clear Yaz is excited about finally getting to be involved with something that's different, yet the audience gets to see her lack of confidence when the Doctor attempts to grill her on how she plans on reporting the incident with the alien on the train, especially when she states she would have to check video footage when she clearly saw what happened literally in front of her own eyes.

In *The Ghost Monument*, Yaz has pretty much given up the authoritative police officer role and has taken a liking to the Doctor, following her orders, and helping out the rest of the gang as much as she can. The audience learns that she has sisters, though they don't always get along. However, Yaz was missing them.

In *Arachnid in the UK*, the audience gets their first opportunity to really learn about Yaz and her family after Yaz expresses home sickness and desires to go back to her real life. But when the moment comes for them all to go their separate ways, Yaz invites her new friends for tea. There, the audience comes across an awkward moment when Yaz's mother asks Yaz bluntly if she's dating Ryan or The Doctor, indicating that Yaz may be struggling with her sexuality. However, Yaz doesn't seem the least bit uncomfortable being asked. In fact, Yaz appears to be more embarrassed by her father who collects trash.

In *Demons of the Punjab*, Yaz gets a history lesson on her own family that she was not in any way prepared for. When her Nan refused to tell her the story behind the watch that she had just gifted her, she felt hurt, making it all about herself instead of considering, for even a brief moment, that there could be a good reason why her Nan didn't want to share the story. She practically begs the Doctor to take her back in time to the origins of the watch and is delighted when the Doctor agrees.

However, what she is about to prepare for is nothing like she expected. At first, she learns her Nan is about to marry someone different than her granddad and is completely against it. It isn't until she actually gets to know her Nan that she discovers that she really loves this different man. By the end of the episode, she not only grew to love her Nan, but also this other man, and feels complete sympathy and understanding why her Nan didn't want to share the story. It was still a memory that was too painful to remember.

When we get to *The Battle of Ranskoor Av Kolos*, we see a Yaz that seems to have come into her own. She is much more confident in herself and her decision making. She encourages the Doctor to make a move that definitely would put them both in danger by removing their neural stimulators and putting them on the Ux's to help save them from Tzim-Sha's influence.

The #NotMyDoctor Movement

"I know, because we're all the same. We want certainty. Security. To believe that people are evil or heroic. But that's not how people are. You want to know the secrets of existence? Start with the mysteries of the heart."
- 13th Doctor

As a *Doctor Who* fan tweeted after Jodie Whittaker's appearance on *Children In Need* aired, "THIS. THIS is why a female doctor is SO important. This is why Jodie Whittaker will always be a legend." Having a role model for little girls these days is so important, especially during a time when politicians and religious right-wing groups are determined to take women's rights away and degrade women so that they are made to feel their only purpose in life is to be a man's property and procreate. When girls are told they can be anything they want to be, having a female play the lead role in *Doctor Who* goes that extra mile in bringing it into reality. When Jodie Whittaker walked out onto the stage, the look on that young girl's face and her cries of excitement said it all.

Being the first woman to play the role hasn't been a smooth ride. There is a whole group of detractors out there who, it would seem, are bent on denigrating Jodie in any way they can. The group has now come to be known by their mantra: #NotMyDoctor. The #NotMyDoctor's have gone to extremes in their efforts. They inundated the *Children In Need* website with insults about Jodie's acting and about Jodie herself. They have even done this to other charitable endeavors that Jodie has been involved in. They insist that having a female play the role of the Doctor has all but destroyed the show and will lead to its demise. But we true fans know otherwise.

Feminism is a word that has been thrown around a lot since Jodie was announced as the next Doctor. There is no real evidence that this played a role in her being chosen. However, that hasn't stopped people from bringing this word up in relation to it. Feminism has been around since the early 60's. Woman's Lib, as it was called at that time, raised a lot of ire from most men and some women. They did not think that women were, or could be, equal to men in any way. This fight is still going strong as is evidenced by those who are so vociferous against Jodie. And I believe it will continue until women are truly equal to men in all aspects of life. It is more important now than ever that we teach girls WHO they are, WHAT they are capable of, and that they can be WHATEVER they want to be in life.

The #NotMyDoctor group seem to have been emboldened by the surge of hate that happened after Donald Trump won the Presidency in 2016. They are now attacking fans of the show. The #NotMyDoctors are not above going to message boards and personally attacking *Doctor Who* fans. They say that if anyone believes that Jodie Whittaker is a good actress or an excellent choice for the role of the Doctor they are 'not true fans of *Doctor Who*' and they should go jump in a lake, so to speak.

This group has started many rumors that have caused waves among the fans of *Doctor Who,* which seems to have further emboldened them. There were rumors that Jodie and Chris Chibnall, the current showrunner, had a falling out on set and Jodie walked off saying she was done. There were rumors of a Christmas special where Jodie's Doctor would regenerate signaling that Jodie would not return for Season 12. The #NotMyDoctor group has even gone so far as to say that David Tennant would be lectured by Jodie about his toxic masculinity and told he HAD to repent for his part in perpetuating it.

If you don't like Jodie or her acting, you are welcome to your opinion. I get it, I really do, because I wasn't so sure about her being the Doctor at first either. But to tell someone else they are not a true fan because they feel differently than you is not acceptable. And, to personally attack someone just because you think they should not play a particular role is even more heinous. The #NotMyDoctor group has done just that. They personally attacked Jodie when she recorded Coldplay's "Yellow" for *Children In Need* and mocked her when she revealed that she chose that song as a tribute to her nephew in heaven. They went on message boards and websites saying things like 'not only can she not act she can't sing either.' If they could put aside their hate long enough to just *listen*, they would know that Jodie is a very good singer.

During the *Children In Need* event, there was a little girl chosen to come on stage who was dealing with self-esteem issues. Through *Children In Need* she had been able to overcome this through acting. She was also a huge *Doctor Who* fan. The *Children in Need* organization was able to arrange for this young girl to meet her hero, Jodie Whittaker. Jodie is one of those actors who is able to really connect with their fans and what it really means to be the Doctor and represent the message behind *Doctor Who*. As I myself suffer from depression and self-esteem issues, I know that that little girl's life has been changed forever. This is so important because for someone who suffers from self-esteem issues, it really only takes one person to help you believe in yourself and make those beliefs become truths.

To show how despicable these #NotMyDoctor people are, they personally attacked the little girl who was brought up on stage to meet Jodie Whittaker. They claim that she was a paid actor. That's right, this little girl was paid to go on stage and *pretend* to be excited to meet Jodie. They attacked the gift that Jodie gave the girl by saying that it was a joke gift, that if the girl was such a fan, she would already have a sonic of her own. But it doesn't stop there. One person claimed that she wasn't a little girl at all. She was in fact a 30 year-old dwarf named Ethel. They also claimed that one of their 'members' was in the audience and that when the cameras were not on the girl, the producers were rubbing onions in her eyes to make her cry. How absurd! The things that these people come up with are completely ridiculous! If the onion thing were true, there would be an outcry about child abuse.

The most recent thing that has come out of these #NotMyDoctor people is from Twitter. It is almost as if these people LIVE on Twitter. They outright attacked a writer of *Doctor Who*. They claimed this particular writer, a woman, is anti-men; she is a feminist and her writing excludes men. They further claimed that her feminism was the reason a male writer was recently fired. Their post was hash tagged with #fireher and #rehirehim.

The funny thing is that this particular woman is not actually a *Doctor Who* writer. She is a member of "The Time Ladies," a *Doctor Who* fan page and website. She is a writer, and outspoken on women's issues. However, her writing was not the reason the man was fired nor did her feminism have anything to do with it. This particular male writer was fired for his transphobic views. As a whole, this group of people have done more to incite the anti-feminist, rumor-mongering, troglodytes than anything the BBC or the writers of *Doctor Who* could have ever done.

On a more positive note the theme that runs through the entire life of the *Doctor Who* television show is inclusiveness. It does not matter who you are, there will be a message for you. White, black, yellow, red or brown, male or female, gay, straight, non-binary or transgender, Christian or Atheist, everyone has a net worth that cannot, and should not, be disregarded. The only political issues that may be covered in any *Doctor Who* script will be there simply to show how those issues are human issues and cannot be attributed to any single group of people. This is a message that is very important in today's world. With a President that appears to make hate acceptable, *Doctor Who* must continue to help show that it is not. Otherwise, we may end up facing the ugly specters of segregation, civil war, and genocide based on religious beliefs or personal identification.

Early Discussion of Series 12

"Is anyone excited? Cause I'm very excited."
- 13th Doctor

After re-watching these episodes, I'm honestly surprised how much more enjoyable I found them than the first time around. I knew what to expect, therefore, I could look deeper into each episode and grow a deeper appreciation and greater understanding of what the producers and writers were trying to say.

I had read on Twitter of several other *Doctor Who* fans reporting similar findings, but I didn't think that would be possible for me without it coming across as biased, especially because I'm writing this book. (Yes, really, nobody hired me to write this book on the requirement I love Jodie Whittaker and her Doctor). Rather, it was more for the fact that I love *Doctor Who*, and that it has played an important role in my life.

Now that I am thinking about it, on a random thought, I suspect history is repeating itself in the *Doctor Who* fandom, and that's why you come across fans who absolutely cannot wrap their heads around the thought the Doctor can be female. They think the Doctor is male and will only ever be male in their mind, and that's okay. Those fans will come around eventually, or they will continue to be lost, and instead, fall into the trap of being a fan of an actor rather a fan of the Doctor.

That being said, I really do hope a majority of the people who are reading this book enjoyed Series 11. Yes, at times it had its flaws, but honestly, I'm glad it wasn't perfect the first time around. That just makes the expectation for Series 12 to be so much greater, and when Chris Chibnall and the rest of the gang return, we'll be even more delighted to know the future of *Doctor Who* is in good hands.

Perhaps, all we really need to do is *trust* the Doctor: "It's such an exciting feeling," said Jodie Whittaker of Series 12, in a brief phone call to the Zoe Ball Breakfast Show on October 4th. "We're coming to the end of shooting, and we're all really, really excited to show it off. There is so much happening, there really is. It's nine wonderful months of running about and coming up against some very exciting monsters along the way. Yeah, it's gonna be great!"

Speaking of, let's take a look into what to expect in Series 12, and some of the rumors that simply, for whatever reason, refuse to die, as well as what I'd like to see happen in the next series: (Note: if you don't want to read any potential spoilers for the next series, skip the rest of this chapter).

What I'd Like to See

The Stenza

In episode called *The Ghost Monument*, we learned the Stenza have been conquering other worlds and forcing other species to build weapons for purposes of genocide. I would like to see a storyline where The Doctor and her companions visit several different planets that have been affected by the Stenza in order to explore how powerful this new alien species is. Would it even be possible for The Doctor to travel back in time to prevent some of these events from occurring or would it simply make things worse?

The Thirteenth Doctor's Theme

I would love for there to be an episode that takes place in Ireland. Maybe during the potato famine? Maybe The Doctor discovers the famine was actually created by aliens? That way the energetic 13th Doctor Celtic theme we hear in both *The Woman Who Fell to Earth* and *The Ghost Monument* would have a bit more of a significance.

The Doctor's Femininity

While we did get to see a glimpse of the challenges The Doctor could face being a woman in *The Witchfinders*, I feel like the show could dive deeper, and explore that topic a bit more without it being overboard. For example, what if The Doctor ended up in a situation where Ryan and Graham were not around, and she struggles to resolve the problem solely because she's a female.

Dark! Doctor

I've seen other works of Jodie Whittaker where she has been absolutely brilliant in her performance that is in the genre of drama. I don't feel like her Doctor has been pushed enough yet. While I do feel the writers are trying to get away from previous incarnations of The Doctor, who identified themselves as an "oncoming storm," but that is an element that I think will always remain with The Doctor. She's seen too much and done too much to not be permanently affected by events of the past.

What We Know

The Judoon

Already previously confirmed this past May by the BBC, fans of *Doctor Who* are looking forward to seeing the return of fan favorite Rhino-headed space cops, the Judoon, for a deadly mission. For those who are not familiar with them, or need a refresher, they are a mercenary species known for their precision and brutality. They have bodies built like humanoids and brains the size of a fist. Their heads are shaped like a rhinoceros. They have lungs, which allow them to survive in environments with limited oxygen supplies, bleed yellow blood and carry weapons next to their heavy black armor that can incinerate a human upon detonation.

The BBC teased *Doctor Who* fans with a photograph from Series 12, where The Doctor, restrained, is staring into the eyes of a Judoon wearing a Mohawk.

"No! Sho! Blo! The Judoon are storming back into *Doctor Who* in full force, and the streets of Gloucester aren't safe," teased Chibnall to the *Radio Times*. "If anyone has anything to hide, confess now. The Judoon are taking no prisoners and will stop at nothing to fulfill their mission! The whole team on *Doctor Who* are delighted and scared in equal measure to welcome them back: one of many treats we've got in store for viewers next series."

It is later teased in the same article that there may be a story involving espionage.

Extended Story for Yaz

Some fans criticized the writers during Series 11 for focusing too much on companions Graham and Ryan, versus, equally balancing out each companion story arcs. At a special screening for *The Doctor Who* New Year's episode, *Resolution*, Chibnall addressed the possibility of a new storyline for Yaz and whether she would ever return back to the Sheffield police force.

"I think that some of these questions may be answered in the forthcoming season," he teased.

The Cybermen

Despite never officially being confirmed by the BBC for Series 12, photographs appeared on Instagram from August 21st and 22nd taken at Nash Point in Wales. Actors dressed as Cybermen, emotionless cyborgs that were once human, but have since been converted to increase their perfection, were identified with what could only be described as a new *upgrade*.

The Cyberman is both a classic *Doctor Who* monster as well as a fan favorite that has made multiple appearances in the show since its revival in 2005. Last time they were seen in an episode of *Doctor Who*, the 12th

Doctor and then companion Bill, were attempting to stop them from a cyber invasion on a Mondasian colony ship.

Additional images from the same location also depicted what looked like part of a medieval set with a campsite, brown tents, constructed on the Wales shoreline. Amongst the photographs were also multiple images of an older actor dressed in brown robes, carrying a wizard staff. The robe specifically had some kind of white colored symbols all over it. How this wizard and the Cyberman are connected storyline wise, if they even are, is unknown.

Speaking of storylines, one of the rumors that has yet to be confirmed states that the storyline may be similar to the tale told in Big Finish Productions audio drama titled *The Silver Turk*, which starred the Eighth Doctor. If the rumors are true, it wouldn't be the first time the show revamped an audio drama for television. The episode, *Dalek*, which appeared as a Ninth Doctor story during Christopher Eccleston's era, was inspired/recreated from Big Finish Productions audio drama, *Jubilee*, which was originally written for the Sixth Doctor.

Another rumor I have heard are these Cybermen will be petrifying 19th century England and helping to inspire author Mary Shelley to write her novel, *Frankenstein*. Whether we should prepare ourselves for a much darker Series 12 in 2020, we'll have to stay tuned.

Doctor Who Christmas Special

One of the treats fans have been able to enjoy throughout most of the modern era of *Doctor Who* is getting to spend time with The Doctor on Christmas.

However, in Series 11, for the first-time fans had to wait until New Year's Day for a special episode, which technically is considered separate.

Fans were hoping Chris Chibnall would bring back the Christmas tradition to *Doctor Who,* but to their disappointment, it was confirmed by *Titan Comics* there would be no Christmas special in 2019.

"There's no BBC Christmas Special this yea—so we're bringing the fans what they want, in comic form!" wrote Titan Comics on their website. "Can The Doctor save Christmas? Is Santa a myth, a man, or a Time Lord? Are chimneys bigger on the inside?! Two-part festive fun from Jody House (Stranger Things, Spider-Man: Renew Your Vows)."

As a result, fans have jumped to the conclusion that there will be another New Year's episode to launch Series 12 instead, which has now been confirmed by the BBC. The new season will premier on New Year's Day.

Daleks

However, there does appear that there will be a Christmas special in 2020, after a document leaked showing Lee Haven Jones directed this specific episode this year. And not only that, but on October 22nd, nine new Daleks were spotted on the Clifton Suspension Bridge in Bristol! Based on the pictures I've seen they have a new black and silver color design. Some fans will say the Daleks have been overdone, but I always get excited when they're around.

Rumors

Jodie Whittaker and Chris Chibnall Leaving

This rumor has been going around for almost a year, thanks to #NotMyDoctor fans, yet has been debunked time and time again by various media outlets as being nothing more than that... a rumor.

Back in November of 2018, *Starburst Magazine* reported an unnamed representative from the BBC had informed them that Chibnall was unhappy with how things were running behind the scenes, and therefore was looking to leave *Doctor Who* after Series 12. It was also reported that Jodie Whittaker would be leaving the show as well at that time due to not being interested in staying in the historic role without Chibnall as showrunner. Bradley, Mandip and Tosin would supposedly be leaving too.

What I gather really happened is this rumor was started as a direct result of what happened before news broke that there was going to be a delay between Series 11 and Series 12. This was something that was not in any shape or form Chibnall's fault. Allegedly, it was reported when the higher ups at the BBC informed Chibnall he would have to delay the next series of the show by a year, he became upset. Honestly, can anyone blame him? I mean, he just had his debut series as showrunner air with record breaking ratings, and now he's being told he has to delay the show? The BBC saw what happened to the ratings when there was a delay during Capaldi's run. It tanked and never recovered.

So, you can almost guarantee from a business perspective, Chibnall had no intention of any kind of delay. In fact, when he was hired as the new showrunner, he promised to have five consecutive years of *Doctor Who* on the air. So now, for those on the outside who do not understand what's really going on behind the scenes, some will get the impression that he's incompetent. And that's exactly what happened, because shortly after the news leaked, fan site *Outpost Skaro* reported that Chibnall told the executives that a "full series-a-year is unsustainable" and that it's too much for Jodie because she's a new young Mum! So, here's an example of how something can be completely blown out of proportion.

Oh, but the rumor didn't end there. It returned back from the dead like the Master (I will discuss that particular Time Lord in this chapter a bit later). One of the most well-known #NotMyDoctor fans, this past August, who is well-known in the fandom for being a Jodie Whittaker hater, stated on their YouTube channel that Chris Chibnall had been fired, which sent Twitter into a frenzy; exactly what this fan wanted.

This time the story was that the BBC had allegedly decided to let Chibnall go after not being happy with the cuts of Series 12 they had received due to it not meeting their guidelines. (This part already was confusing because as far as Series 12 was concerned, it was still filming).

Peter McTighe had been hired as temporary showrunner. To make things worse, reports were stating a group of people had sued the BBC for lost wages due to not having a consistent run of *Doctor Who* every year for five years as promised, and Jodie Whittaker had walked off set, but had agreed to a Christmas 2020 regeneration scene. While BBC never did release a statement to confirm or deny these rumors, and they honestly won't because they generally do not comment on rumors, multiple other resources such as *The Radio Times*, for example, have gone on to say none of it is true. Nonetheless, this is one rumor that simply refuses to die.

Rose Tyler Returning

Around this time last year, a rumor started that Chris Chibnall and Matt Strevens were in early talks to bring beloved fan favorite actress, Billie Piper, back to the show to reprise her role as Rose Tyler. Fans who had voiced displeasure about the story writing in Series 11 became excited at the notion that Rose may be returning. Even Jodie Whittaker herself had voiced at San Diego Comic Con she would love to work with Billie Piper.

Not much more was said about this rumor until May of 2019 when Billie posted on her social media platforms that there was going to be a huge announcement. This again caused many fans to believe that she was returning to the show, and it turned out her character was, in a way, but not how fans expected. Big Finish Productions, the company who makes *Doctor Who* audio dramas, created a new special release called *Rose Tyler: The Dimension*

Cannon, which would follow Rose on her return journey from Pete's world back to The Doctor's world.

A Tenth Doctor and Thirteenth Doctor Story

In mid-August, a picture appeared on Instagram of Jodie Whittaker and David Tennant hanging out together. It was speculated by fans that *Doctor Who* was cooking up another multi-Doctor story, this time featuring the 10th and 13th Doctors. Turns out, they were working on a singing project together for *Children In Need*. The album is currently available to listen on Spotify and will be available to purchase soon on other platforms. All proceeds will go to the charity.

Also, at this year's New York Comic Con, news dropped from Titan Comics that an upcoming storyline in the 13th Doctor comics will feature the 10th Doctor, as they collaborate together to defeat another fan favorite monster, the Weeping Angels.

The Master

The Master is another Time Lord from Gallifrey, who in early story lines was intended to be The Doctor's brother, but that never actually happened due to the sudden passing of actor Roger Delgado, who played the first incarnation of the Master (1971-1973). He was filming a mini-series in Turkey when the vehicle he was traveling in, along with two Turkish film technicians, abruptly went into a ravine. Later, Jon Pertwee who portrayed the Third incarnation of

The Doctor, admitted Delgado's death played a factor in his decision to leave *Doctor Who*.

The Master is the opposite to The Doctor, yet over time, has played the role of both the friend and the enemy. Last time the audience had seen the Master (then going by the name Missy, short for The Mistress, played by actress Michelle Gomez during Peter Capaldi's era), she had been stabbed and killed by her previous, male incarnation (being played by John Simm).

I've honestly lost count how many times the Master has "died" yet somehow always manages to return, so it really shouldn't be a surprise to viewers when his/her name starts floating around.

This past summer, a rumor started going around stating that the Master will be returning in a new male incarnation in Series 12, and will be played by actor Sacha Dhawan, who *Doctor Who* fans would best recognize from playing director Waris Hussein in *An Adventure in Space and Time*. He also previously worked on *The Wire* alongside Jodie Whittaker.

I haven't come across anything further since this rumor first started, however, I did manage to get blocked on Twitter by an angry *Doctor Who* fan because I dared to comment on someone else's thread on the topic.

Sea Devils

Another rumor that's been going around the internet is a storyline apparently involving Florence Nightingale, the 13th Doctor and the Sea Devils. The Sea Devils are related to the Silurians, an ancient race who once ruled the earth when humans were still considered apes. The Sea Devils are the Silurians' cousins. Both the Sea Devils and the Silurians went into hibernation, the Sea Devils under the ocean, and the Silurians, underground, due to the belief of an extinction event that their scientists warned would occur. It's possible this same extinction event was the same one that killed off the dinosaurs.

However, for both of their species, this extinction event never happened, and by the time they came out of hibernation, humans had evolved. This made them terribly angry and they decided to take the Earth back. This is when they first met The Doctor. The Doctor has tried in the past to negotiate a peaceful treaty so both Silurian and Human can walk the surface of the Earth together. The Master has also encountered the Sea Devils before, so perhaps there is some truth behind the rumor returning. If not, perhaps Jodie's Doctor will be successful in creating a peaceful treaty if she encounters this mysterious ancient race.

Doctor/Yaz

Chris Chibnall promised there would not to be any hanky panky in the TARDIS in Series 11. However, many fans have come aware of the close, real life friendship that has developed between Jodie Whittaker and Mandip Gill, that some fans have taken it so far to believe the writers are going to make them a couple. More than likely that will not happen, but until it's proven right or wrong, this remains a rumor.

River Song

When Alex Kingston was asked at Wales Comic Con by a fan on whether River Song would be returning to the new series of *Doctor Who*, she said, "Spoilers! I can't say anything yet, but you will be in for a big surprise!" Could this mean she will be returning or is merely throwing off the fans? I can confirm she will be returning in 2020 for another entry in The Diary of River Song series from Big Finish Productions where River will be taking on the Weeping Angels.

The Writing

The last significant rumor that is still floating around surrounds the writing team. Some fans have voiced their displeasure in the writing, criticizing it be too PC and leftist. The latest rumor states that Chris Chibnall has decided to go back to the style of other former showrunners, such as Russell T. Davies, by having a mix of stand-alone episodes mixed with two-parters that have an arc, which connects the entire series. Neither the BBC nor has Chris Chibnall confirmed or denied this intention. This is something that, again, we'll just have to wait and see.

Interviews

"Enough questions. You lot, you love to chat, I get it. Lots to do. I'm working on it all… Give me nine minutes, a bit of quiet, and I'll be ready to roll. Scout's honor."
- 13th Doctor

Here you can read exclusive, never before printed interviews with people who either currently work on the show or contribute something very significant towards the show. You may even learn a new thing or two!

Wendy Abrahams
Beth Axford
Christian Basel
Will Brooks
Ken Deep
Stephen Hatcher
Krystal Moore
Alisa Stern

Wendy Abrahams:
a Jodie Whittaker Impressionist

That was the voice of brilliant Wendy Abrahams featured at the beginning of my book trailer. Can you tell me a little bit about your acting background?

I was trained in Musical theater, then worked as a showgirl in Malta and Ibiza and I even sang on the ocean liner—the QE2. I then moved into British Vaudeville working as a ventriloquist. When I met my partner (fellow impressionist Wink Taylor) I then moved into presenting and magic.

Were voice impersonations something you could always do, or did you have to learn it?

I've always loved performing different accents and making my family laugh by devising up different characters.

Who was your first voice impersonation?

I never really used to impersonate celebrities; it was mainly dialects.

What interested you in studying Jodie Whittaker's voice?

Jodie's voice is fascinating, because it is quite deep and heavily accented. She is from the North of England where the vowel sounds are quite unusual. It is a pleasure to impersonate her.

Were you a fan of hers before she became the 13th Doctor?

Very much so! She was the absolute star of the series *Broadchurch* which was a ratings smash in the U.K. I was hooked on not only the show, but her performance in particular.

Congratulations on being recognized for your 13th Doctor impersonation by the Radio Times! How did the Ode to a Timelord project come about?

Mr. Luke Oliver, who devised the entire project, had used Wink's voice for Sylvester McCoy and Peter Davison. When he had said to Wink that he was struggling to find a Jodie impersonator, Wink volunteered me, and before I knew it—I was on board. It was a pleasure to be involved in such a quality fan project and it seemed to create a real impact. Luke is fantastic and he assembled an amazing cast. I really hope I can work with him again.

In April of 2018, you made a tribute video to the thrilling Thirteenth Doctor. How did you go about recreating the introduction trailer scene?

I loved making that video. I thought the way Jodie was announced was fantastic and utterly unique. I watched that footage so many times and this was before I could do the impression of her. I filmed my tribute on green screen and spent quite some time making certain the camera angle and the action matched the original footage. Of course, the big difference was Jodie wasn't interrupted by a very silly puppet! Great fun.

Have you ever gotten the lucky chance to meet her before? Has she heard your impression?

I have not met Jodie (yet!) but I really hope I get the chance to do so. I hope she likes my impression of her, which is intended as a tribute rather than a parody. I've been quite lucky as I have met Colin, Sylvester, Christopher Eccleston and David Tennant. I am also very good friends with Matt Smith's acting double who is a drummer in a band I sing with. I have also had a Terrileptil and a Tetrap stay in my home and regularly work with an Ood. (All true!)

If an opportunity to do an audiobook came about, is that something you would be interested in?

Oh definitely. I love audio drama!

Besides doing impersonations of Jodie Whittaker, you also do a show called Theo the Mouse. Considering there are many readers of this book who are American *Doctor Who* fans, can you share what your show is all about? What has been your favorite Theo the Mouse episode?

Theo The Mouse is a puppet character (voiced and operated by Wink Taylor) who is very much inspired by the world of Jim Henson—the U.S. genius behind the Muppets. Performing with Theo is an absolute joy, because he appeals to all ages, so we have quite a large demographic within our audience. My favorite time of year is Christmas, so the Theo The Mouse Christmas Show is the one I love performing the most. Theo is quite a Who fan and the eagle-eyed fans often spot *Doctor Who* references in his scripts!

I noticed that Theo the Mouse appears at UK Holidayparks. Since, I am not familiar with that term, is that what Americans would call a theme park-like Bush Gardens, Six Flags, Cedar Point? Or is it more like a carnival?

The Theo The Mouse Show is regularly employed by a company called Butlins. I suppose the closest U.S. equivalent is Coney Island which also has large shows and Carnival Rides for holiday makers. Butlins is a British institution and most people in the U.K. have been there or know people who have. Some of our biggest British performers have entertained there, and it is an honor to be part of that tradition.

Are there any other acting projects you are currently involved in?

Yes! I have a number of Jodie projects which I am very excited about and the Theo The Mouse Show changes every year, so repeat audiences always see a different show. I also sing in a number of bands and am always learning new songs.

How can people find out more about you?

You can always check out the Theo The Mouse Facebook Page and follow @TheoMouse on Twitter. (May I take this opportunity to wish Mackenzie Flohr all the best with her excellent book and thank her for using my vocal tribute to Jodie to help promote it).

Beth Axford from *The Time Ladies*

As a fan, I first encountered you through The Time Ladies. Can you share what your website is about for those who are just joining the fandom or may have never visited your site?

Our website (and now podcast, YouTube and social media channels) aims to be a space for all *Doctor Who* fans from the perspective of female, trans and nonbinary fans of the show. We try to give platforms to women, trans and nonbinary people who may not otherwise be able to get their voices heard in a very male-dominated space. Our content ranges from covering and reviewing the show and its products to opinion pieces, fashion guides and make-up tutorials. There is, we hope, something for everyone.

Congratulations on being selected to be part of *Doctor Who Magazine's* Time Team! How did that come about?

I was asked to be on the Time Team around March of last year. Basically, Benjamin Cook (who wrote and collated our thoughts for the article) had seen some of the Time Ladies content and thought both Kezia and I would be great for the team. His aim was to get as many young, diverse voices as possible, so he really wanted some women involved giving a different perspective on *Doctor Who*.

Can you share with me a special moment or perhaps something funny with the Time Team that you haven't shared on social media or the Time Ladies?

Every moment doing the Time Team felt special and meant a lot to me. I think one of the funniest moments that I don't think I have mentioned is when we were walking down the red carpet for the Series 11 premiere, and Tosin Cole recognized Miles. They began chatting like old friends and we all stood there astonished. It turns out that they both went to acting school together years ago and Tosin remembered Miles from there. It was a lovely moment and I don't think Miles even thought for a second that Tosin would recognize him—he hadn't even told us they went to school together!

You also got to be one of the lucky ones chosen to see Season 11's special premiere in Sheffield, correct? Did you get the opportunity to meet Jodie? If so, what was she like?

Yes, we were very lucky to be invited to the series 11 premiere—it was very intimate and there wasn't a lot of press invited. We met Jodie after we viewed the episode, which made it all the more special because it was truly an incredible story that made me cry so many times—just seeing a woman playing The Doctor, and Jodie doing it so fantastically—It was Kezia and I who found her hiding out waiting to leave. We didn't want to bother her, but she was very happy to chat and have a photo. We told her about the Time

Ladies and thanked her for taking on the role. I'd love to meet her again and have a good old chin wag!

What was your reaction to Jodie Whittaker's casting as The Doctor?

My reaction was complete astonishment that the BBC had finally given the role to a woman. I also never used to be a fan of the idea years ago, but when it came to a new Doctor being announced I just couldn't see them being male—it was always a woman in my mind. I have no idea why. It just felt right! When the reveal happened, I finally felt a sense of relief and acceptance that someone like me was about to become The Doctor and that feeling stays with me constantly.

Honestly, do you think she'll ever be able to convince the #NotMyDoctor fans that she really IS The Doctor and The Doctor CAN be female?

I think quite honestly that nothing will ever change the minds of the 'Not my Doctor' crowd. They seem to be stuck in their own way and unable to empathize or see anything from anyone's perspective but their own. It is difficult to deal with, and sad that they are unable to accept a woman. The problem is that the world will move on and equality will be reached at some point and once all this happens, they will be left in the dark. You have to grow and change, or you will get left behind!

Season 11's theme was about inclusivity and representation for all. How important do you feel that is for *Doctor Who* at this time?

I think it's incredibly important that *Doctor Who* surrounds itself with inclusivity. Not only because it is doing the very basic thing of just portraying how the world is around us, but because it is primarily a children's show. It is supposed to educate and show us that anyone can be the hero, that anyone can be in the TARDIS team. I don't see how it is supposed to fulfill its purpose as a show and franchise without being inclusive and progressive.

Some fans accused the show of being too PC. Did at any time you feel that it was? If so, what could the show have done better?

I don't think the show is 'too PC.' That's like saying the world we live in is 'too PC.' As Mandip Gill says—when people say 'too PC,' are they trying to insinuate that people's lives and culture and history are just acts of political correctness? No. These stories are real, and they are a part of people's lives. Basic human rights and inclusivity are not too politically correct.

What are some of the things you'd like the show do next?

I would like the show to focus a little more on Yaz's character, as they gave a lot to Ryan and Graham in 11. If we're talking further into the future, I'd love more body inclusion in the show, and representation of trans people. Some new creatures and aliens are always fun, and I love everything *Doctor Who* has to offer, but it's those personal touches and seeing different perspectives on screen that I always look for.

If you could write a novel, audio or even an episode for *Doctor Who*, which would you prefer and why?

I would love to do an audio, novel or episode—
I'd be incredibly honored to do any of them! It is a
personal goal of mine though to write a *Doctor Who*
novel. I don't know if it is because it seems more
attainable than an episode or just because it fits my
writing style more. I grew up spending hours pouring
over and reading *Doctor Who* books and it is one of
the reasons I so badly wanted to become a writer.

**Recently you wrote an article about how The
Doctor has been able to help people with mental
illness. What would your advice be to a fan who
may be struggling?**

There is so much advice out there, I don't know if
anything I could say would be able to help. But my
advice would be to look after yourself as best as you
can. Do everything you can, even though it feels
impossible. Talk about it as much as you can, tell your
friends and family. Write things down, get them out.
Find a passion and use it to fuel you. This is why
Doctor Who, writing and The Time Ladies have been
so beneficial to me—they are things that distract me
and pull me up a bit out of that darkness.

**Seriously, Comic Con. Am I ever going to see you
there as a guest? Like Gallifrey One?**

GOD. It is my life goal to go to Gallifrey One,
especially now Eccleston is going. It is just super
expensive though and I don't know where I would find
the money. I will be participating in some *Doctor Who*
stuff for London Comic Con, so maybe one day
Gallifrey One? And of course, I'd love to meet you!

How can people find out more about you?

You can follow the Time Ladies on Twitter/IG/Facebook or go to thetimeladies.com and I tweet a lot about my more personal *Doctor Who* stuff @0hmyst4rs! Our podcast 'Time Ladies Talk' is on iTunes and Soundcloud and Spotify.

Christian Basel: Host of *The Legend of the Traveling TARDIS* Radio Show

How did your podcast get started?

I was leaving another podcast called Gallifrey Stands. It was a mutual break up. Nothing bad. Iain Shaw, who runs the podcast, lives in the UK and I live in the US and our schedules made it impossible to sync up to do episodes together. So, I left. I told my current boss from the Hangin' with Web Show, Garrett Pomichter, what had happened, and he just replied, "it's time." He said that I was ready to go on my own. I didn't. It took some convincing from Garrett and I finally agreed. Before this, I had been off and on podcasts for the last seven years, including the Hangin' with Web Show. Then, we set the date, October 6th, 2018. The day before Jodie Whittaker was to premiere as The Doctor, we premiered. And the rest is radio show history.

For the person who has never listened to your show before, what kind of topics do you discuss?

Of course, *Doctor WHO*. But I wanted to delve into issues that were more than just reviews of an episode. I wanted to explore topics that I wanted to dive into that I wasn't hearing on the other shows.

What makes your podcast different from others?

I have an awesome team who have a lot to contribute to the show. It started with three people and has grown into a radio show family. Also, I wanted to bring up topics that I don't hear about on the other shows much that I wanted to address like bullying in the WHOniverse. Topics that go beyond characterization and stories. I believe if it's something worthy of talking about, the audience will listen. And I always want our listeners to have fun.

How do you determine the topic of each podcast episode?

Sometimes, they're usually just things pop in the back of my mind. Something that I heard someone discuss. Usually, my teammates will come up with something.

Any particular problems have you encountered trying to put your show together?

I think any radio show has their technical issues and so on, but with this radio show family, I have no issues. A lot of things have fallen into place.

What are your thoughts on Jodie Whittaker and her 13th Doctor?

For me, she's currently untapped potential. Jodie is a terrific actress, there is no doubt about it, but I think the way that Chris Chibnall has directed her, he's not using her acting abilities to her full capacity. I've seen her in *Broadchurch* and Attack the Block. If Chibnall can show me the "Space God" inside her, I'm all in.

Where do you picture the podcast being in five years?

I really don't know. I do have goals that we have met along the way in leaps and bounds. We became part of the iHeart Radio family within two months of our premiere. I still remember the call. Garrett telling me this on Christmas Eve. It was the best Christmas present of 2018. Then, we became part of CBS Radio's Radio.com. That was my 2019 New Year's present. Ultimately, I would love every WHOvian out there to listen to our show. I think we're off to a good start.

Podcasts often times get a vendor table at comic con. Is that something you'd like to do with other *Doctor Who* conventions particularly?

Who wouldn't?

Do you have a favorite memory from any of your episodes? What was it?

Each episode has a place in my heart, but my fondest memory is our first episode. Where it all began. I was nervous.

Who is your favorite guest that has been on the show?

I know this sounds like a cop out, but I've enjoyed them all. Each one of them has made a terrific contribution to the show, and some like Simon Fisher-Becker, have stayed on to be part of the radio show family.

If you could have anybody on your podcast, who would you want to invite that you haven't yet?

Everyone. Personally, I'd love to have Peter Capaldi, but I want everyone.

What's the worst error you have made on air?
Take your pick LOL!

How can people find out more about your podcast?
The best place to get started is on TheLegendOfTheTravelingTARDIS.com. We also drop episodes weekly on our social medias which include Facebook, Twitter and Instagram. You could basically Google search us by name and find us on places like iHeart Radio, iTunes, Spreaker, Krypton Radio, Podbean, the list goes on where people can listen and subscribe.

Interview with Will Brooks

I want to start off this interview by congratulating Will on the birth of his child! Can you tell me a bit of your background?

Ah, thank you! As for my background... I've always been 'creative.' As a kid my favorite book was called *101 Things to Do With Cardboard*, and I was basically glued to it (thanks to an accident while attempting thing number 72). I used to buy *Smash Hits* magazine every week, cut out the images—mostly of the Spice Girls—and cellotape them to little index cards to make my own magazine covers. The irony of that being basically what I've done for the last five years for the covers of the comics isn't lost on me!

At university I studied Film and Television Production, but it was never really what I fancied doing—I simply reached 18 and needed to pick a subject to study! I spent three years on that, including an afternoon working on the children's television program *Blue Peter*, which I think was the most stressful day of my life! I left Television Centre in London that day and vowed to never set foot in a TV studio again. I've not quite managed to keep that promise to myself, but I've never technically worked in TV again!

After a couple of years designing kitchens, I decided that I wanted to try my hand at a bit of artwork and graphic design, so went freelance in 2013 and started to pick up work from there. My first clients were The Doctor Who Experience in Cardiff Bay, where I was living at the time, and I've continued in much that same direction for the last five years.

When I starting to do research for this book series, I stumbled upon your eighth Doctor poster. Were you always a fan of *Doctor Who*?

Thanks to some detective work from people on Twitter a few months ago, I can pinpoint my first exposure to *Doctor Who* as being in January 1998, when Channel 4 in the UK showed the second Peter Cushing film.

I didn't really get into it for another five years, though. At the tail end of 2003 I stumbled on the then-recently released VHS of *Invasion of the Dinosaurs* at the local library. I remember thinking that *Doctor Who* was something to do with time travel, and that the blurb to the tape sounded brilliant, so I rented it out.

Over the next year or so I picked up a few of the DVDs—*The Tomb of the Cybermen* and *Resurrection of the Daleks* I definitely remember, but I'm sure there were a few more—and I thought it was pretty cool. It wasn't until the series returned to screens in 2005 with Christopher Eccleston and Rose that I really became a FAN. Because I'd not really been following it, I'd sort of missed that it was coming back until the day of broadcast. Then all of a sudden there was brand new Doctor! That's the best feeling in the world. I've never looked back!

How did you get involved with the show in graphic design?

I sort of stumbled into it, really. I'd been doing (some pretty dreadful) fan art for several years, and I'd done some writing for Cubicle 7's Doctor Who Role Playing Game books, but I had no idea how to actually turn all of that into an actual proper job. It was more luck than anything—the day after I left my kitchen design job to go freelance (literally the day after, it couldn't have been more perfect for an anecdote!) I got a call from a friend to say that he was in a meeting at The Doctor Who Experience, and would I pop over to see them. He introduced me to the management as the person who'd be doing all the design on a range of new merchandise they'd just agreed to produce. It was luck more than anything.

While we were working on that throughout 2014, I was doing little bits and pieces for Big Finish on behalf of another friend who was a regular cover artist for them. He'd simply got too much work on and couldn't keep up, so he'd brung me some money here and there to prepare bits for him. Colorize a black and white photo here, cut out some images there, put the covers roughly together as a starting point, that sort of thing. Little tasks which would make the project a bit quicker for him. At the end of that year he'd been asked to do a trilogy of releases for the Fifth *Doctor Who*, and had absolutely no time, so passed my details onto them, and I took over that commission. I did a few covers for them then throughout 2015, and then I got talking to Titan Comics who'd taken over the license to do *Doctor Who* titles for the American market. They mentioned needing someone to do a regular digital art, or photo, cover for each issue, and I commented that the quality of the covers they'd done in that vein so far weren't very good. I thought I'd put my foot in it when the editor then admitted that he'd been putting those together as they didn't have anyone to do it!

They took me on right away and I became the regular 'B Cover' artist for them for about four years. In my time with Titan I think I did just over 200 covers, though that figure also includes some work on Torchwood, Sherlock, Rivers of London, and Penny Dreadful. At one stage around 2016 I was doing something like eight covers a month for them, which was so much fun, but exhausting at the same time! Once the ranges began to slow down through 2017 and 2018, I started to find time for some more Big Finish covers and alternated between the two for a while.

Tell me a bit of the process that goes into making your cover designs. Do you have a stock of photos that you have special access to?

The photos for *Doctor Who* have become something of my specialist subject, though I'm far more an expert on the material from the 21st century era than the 'classic' series. They take thousands and thousands of images during the production of the show—posed photographs of the actors against plain backgrounds (these are the ones I tended to use the most), photos of scenes being performed, behind the scenes shots… so many photos.

The BBC provided me with lots of these, but they don't hold on to everything, so over several years I tracked down thousands of images that had been deleted and lost from their servers. Often, it meant asking the original photographers to dig around for their old hard drives for me. The one shoot I was very keen to find was the shots of David Tennant from *The Runaway Bride*. They'd produced a number of posters in 2006 to promote the episode which showed Tennant pulling some brilliant poses, but no one ever seemed to have the images. The BBC didn't have copies, and *Doctor Who Magazine* didn't have them. I checked in with the brilliant Stuart Crouch who'd used one of their images on a Blu Ray cover a couple of years earlier, but he admitted that he'd not been able to find them either and had resorted to using one of the 2006 posters, and spending hours painting out the show effect that covered Tennant on that image!

Ultimately, Steve Brown, who took the photos, managed to find the original memory cards from the camera for me and sent them over. There wasn't any interest in anyone taking copies when I asked, so I think now the only place those files exist are with me…!

Does Titan Comics come to you with an idea and you take it from there?

I'm a bit dreadful when I'm given a brief. In the early days of my work with Titan, Andrew James, the editor, would send me a proper pitch of what he'd like for the cover… and every single time I'd ignore it! It wasn't a conscious 'I don't want to do that,' it was just a case of my imagination taking it off in a different direction. After a while he stopped giving me briefs, and he'd simply say, "We need a `10th *Doctor Who* cover, two for the 11th *Doctor Who*, and a 12th *Doctor Who* one," and I'd take it from there. Occasionally he'd ask for something specific, if the issue was to feature a returning monster or character, but mostly I was allowed to just get on with it and do what I fancied from issue to issue.

Over time the cover work got quite far ahead of the issues themselves—with the 13th *Doctor Who* for example, I was producing the covers sometimes a year before they'd be released, and several months before the script had been written, so they became a little more generic as we'd never know what would be in the issues. Very few of my ideas got rejected, I think. There were one or two which were dropped because of rights issues with various aliens, and the BBC didn't like a cover I did featuring the Curator from Day of The Doctor posed with an older Sarah Jane Smith from The Sarah Jane Adventures as they felt it implied too strongly that the Curator was *Doctor Who*.

Is the process similar with Big Finish Productions?

With Big Finish, the lead times for the production of an audio drama are far longer than the production of a comic. That means that by the time you're asked to do the cover, there's almost always a script to read if not an entire audio fully recorded! Big Finish have a slightly different style to the comics, so there's always that guideline, and then you can read the script and see what jumps out.

I tended to print out the script and read through it with a highlighter, marking out things that I think might be good to feature on the cover. Then it tends to be a process of trying to find images of the specific *Doctor Who* or companions that are in the story. There's only so many images from the 'classic' series, and with the hundreds of releases Big Finish have done over the years it can be tricky to find new ones, but it's always worth it to make the cover stand out as a bit different!

What is the typical time frame for you to go from design concept to the finished piece?

It varies from piece to piece. Sometimes (the best times!) it'll come together over a few hours in a single afternoon (or, more likely, over a few hours in the middle of the night). Other times it can drag on for days or weeks or even months. I think the hardest thing to learn has been when to keep working at a design and when to accept that it's just not working and it's time to drop it and try something different.

Do you have a favorite piece that you have designed? If so, what? Can you share a story about it?

Almost without exception, my favorite piece of work is whichever piece I've just finished. It tends to be my favorite for a bit and then I'll do something else and that will take over as the favorite. The hardest thing is that because I'm usually working so far ahead of people seeing the work, I'm very, very excited by my new favorite but can't show anyone! That took some getting used to in the early days, and it's still a struggle now!

How much time in advance do you get to create your covers?

Sometimes there's a good long lead time—there's almost always a good month or maybe longer to work on something, but I find I tend to work best when it's a last-minute panic piece. The last cover I did for Titan was the holiday special for 2019, and that one was a case of being emailed on a Monday asking if I'd be able to do it, and telling me that they'd need it ready to submit to approvals by the Wednesday lunchtime. Those are my favorites to do because there's no time to worry about going this way or that way, you just have to sit down and get on with it, and then tends to focus my slightly mad creative mind.

What skills should someone wanting to create design covers learn? Any particular programs, such as Photoshop, they should master?

I think the best skill to learn is just patience. Patience to keep on at it, to keep working and learning. I didn't study design, and I taught myself to use the likes of Photoshop, InDesign, and Illustrator. But I'm still learning every day. I'm constantly realizing that I've been doing things the long-winded way for years, when there's a quick shortcut that achieves the same result!

As an author I have to put my product through an editing process. Is this true of cover design art as well?

It is—once I've done the cover, it goes through to the editor of the comics, or the producer of the audio, then onto their editor or producer, and from there it has to be approved by the BBC, and occasionally by the actors themselves, so it tends to go through several layers of editing.

Has any actor/actress expressed disappointment in how you depicted them in your drawing?

There was an incident very early on, in one of the first bits of design work I did, where a character featured in a story was supposed to be around 30 years younger than they were in the pictures I'd been supplied with, so I Photoshopped them to look younger. Photos from the same shoot had been used previously to depict the character at their present age, so I felt it would be strange to have them looking the same three decades earlier! Unfortunately, I think I caused some offense when that cover went through to be approved, and the actor thought that a comment was being made about their appearance! Luckily, it was all resolved, and a compromise was reached. I actually met said actor years later when we were both guests at the same convention, and they said they knew of the cover and spoke about how much they liked the finished piece, so thankfully no hard feelings there!

We had another actor on another project who I had to deal with several times, and they were always a nightmare. The images used of them had already been through one round of approvals before they were sent to me, but every cover that featured them bounced back three, four, five times as they asked for minor changes. Could their eyebrow be a little more shaped on the left side? They didn't like the way the light sat on their cheek in that shot. The jacket color didn't suit their completion, and they'd like it changed. It seemed to go on forever!

Oh, and actually, I've just remembered another incident, where an actor at a convention was telling me how much they liked my work, and how pleased they were that I did it. We chatted for a while, and they brought up some of the designs they loved. It was all very lovely, until they said how much better my work was than the worst piece they'd ever seen. They proceeded to describe a cover which I recognized as being one of mine, and I had to play dumb about it and say I didn't know who'd done that one!

How can people find out more about you and your work?

The best place tends to be Twitter, where I tweet as @willbrooks1989. I've various other social media which I'm slowly winding down as I move on into my next adventure, but Twitter seems to be the one thing I can't ever give up—I've too many friends on there who I'd miss interacting with!

Ken Deep: Showrunner of L.I. Con

How did your convention get started?

Just after New Year's Day 2013 one of my friends (now business partner in L.I. Who) was hosting her annual holiday party. It had been delayed that year due to the inclement weather we had been experiencing that winter. At this gathering we were lamenting that there were no *Doctor Who* conventions in the New York area. London was set to host a massive 50th anniversary event that November and here in the states Los Angeles and Chicago had long established conventions which I really enjoyed. When we discussed the possibility of doing our own *Doctor Who* convention on Long Island, we realized that we actually had all of the elements we needed to run an event. I looked around the room and asked, "Well, if it's not us, who's it going to be?" Our group was filled with people who had some experience running either conventions or live events, travel and hotel experience, finance, etc. I realized we had all of the elements we needed to run our own convention. That week we formed a business, booked a date at a local hotel, and started inviting guests.

For the person who has never attended comic con, can you describe what your convention is like?

205

We are the opposite of comic con. Big conventions like that have their merit, but I don't enjoy giant events like that. I prefer more intimate, fan run conventions. I really enjoy hotel cons. Holding a convention in a hotel allows attendees to immerse themselves in the experience. It's also more comfortable. You can retreat to your room for some quiet time, or a nap, or just to drop off your big purchase from the vendor hall. I also find that fan run conventions are more customer service oriented. A fan knows what another fan wants and sympathizes with them. There's a bond between us fans. Big events are run by corporations and paid employees. There is definitely a different feel to them.

Any tips or advice for the first-time convention attendee?

Stay hydrated! Wear comfortable shoes and be aware of your hygiene because other humans are attending too. Get as much information prior to the show i.e. schedules, FAQs, and so on. It will save you a lot of time. Book in advance. Buying your admission or add-ons ahead of the convention saves you time and actually helps the con by getting much needed revenue to them during the run up.

For those who have attended before, is there anything new they can expect to see?

I think good convention organizers are always challenging themselves to create something new and exciting every year. I dislike hearing the phrase "Well that's just how we've always done it." In 2019 we've added two paint and sip add-ons that include some of our guests. Attendees will enjoy painting their own *Doctor Who*-themed artwork alongside a guest that they know and love. It's a hands-on activity with a souvenir they get to take home.

What makes your convention different from others?

It's the atmosphere. We really try to create a fun, safe gathering of like-minded friends. It really is a wonderful community. We have folks who have met and fallen in love at our events. Lifelong friendships are often made. I'm most proud of that.

What are your thoughts on the struggles of *Doctor Who* Conventions?

Again, I will encourage you to support your fan run conventions. We will be here supporting your fandom long after the corporate cons are done and have moved on to the next big thing. *Doctor Who* fandom has waxed and waned over the years. It would be impossible for a show with the incredibly long history that *Doctor Who* has not to have ups and downs in popularity. *Doctor Who* conventions will adapt even if we don't have the big budget of previous years.

What particular problems have you encountered trying to put your show together?

Let me start with the first 100! When I began, I thought "How hard could this be?" It's been the biggest challenge of my life. We work almost a full year planning and producing our conventions. There are things I was never expecting to be part of my job when I began. I've learned about the hotel and travel business, for example. I've had to address some uncomfortable behavior one year. Making rules isn't something I'm interested in, but they became necessary. There isn't a day that goes by that I'm not asked to make a difficult decision. I'm sure that the same can be said by any of my fellow convention runners.

Being on Long Island, has your convention ever run into severe weather issues, which has caused the convention to be canceled?

So far... no. It is a factor in picking a date for an event. One of a thousand considerations.

Do you have a favorite memory from any of your conventions and what was it?

Yes, it was November 2016 and we had three of The Doctors at the convention that year. Paul McGann, Peter Davison, and Colin Baker were doing a joint autograph signing session. I was asked by the father of a young lady with special needs to help her meet the three Doctors. We paused the line of attendees waiting to get their autographs so this anxious girl would be less nervous. She met and embraced each of the actors. One by one they spent time talking and getting to know her. Her face was beaming with a smile that my words will fail to illustrate. Her eyes were filled with tears of joy. I have never seen someone so excited in my life. I thought to myself "this made it all worthwhile." I'm proud of my fellow fans who were held up on the line that day. No one complained. In fact, the opposite occurred as many shared in her joy. It's hard as a human being not to feel something when witnessing a moment like that.

Who is your favorite guest that has attended your convention?

That's like asking, "who is your favorite child?" I'm too good a politician to answer.

If money wasn't a factor, who is your ideal guest you'd want to invite that you haven't yet?

Tom Baker. He's the holy grail of *Doctor Who* guests for U.S. promoters since he doesn't travel anymore.

What's the most unusual experience that ever happened at one of your conventions?

My children's programming director almost set the hotel on fire when a toaster oven she was using caught fire. They had been making Shrinky Dinks and the oven overheated. She thought fast and ran the blazing appliance out the door before disaster struck.

How can people find out more about your convention?

Longislanddoctorwho.com or on social media.

Stephen Hatcher:
Showrunner of *Whooverville*

How did Whooverville get started?

The Whoovers fan group had been going for 10 years and we had been holding regular meetings with special guests for almost eight years. Over that time, we had made a few contacts with interesting guests and had often talked about doing a convention. A group of us had crewed at Tenth Planet's Bad Wolf convention, when it came to (nearly) our home territory of Stoke-on-Trent in 2006 and I became a Tenth Planet regular after then, becoming friends with the splendid Derek Hambly. In 2008, Rob Cope of Colin Baker Online asked us to co-organize with him an event at the Gladstone Pottery Museum, also in Stoke, which featured Colin, Rob Shearman and Terry Molloy, and which went very well. In many respects these were the dress rehearsals for Whooverville.

We had gained a bit of experience, but we now wanted to organize our own event, which we called Whooverville. Incidentally it took us about 30 seconds to choose that name, at least three of us suggesting it simultaneously. The problem was that we couldn't afford it. So, we came up with a scheme.

One of our members, Ian Farrington, who by then

had moved to London to work with Big Finish, had a relative who was working at The Midland Railway, a steam/heritage railway north of Derby, and told us that they were looking to host an event, having lost the rights to do Thomas the Tank Engine at that time. We arranged a meeting and my dear friend, the late Robbie Langton, and I went up and made what I thought was a cheeky proposal. We would organize a one-day convention for them, to be held in the engine shed at their lovely site at Swanwick, they would sell the tickets and keep the profits, but they would pay for the event—guests' fees, expenses, the lot. Somewhat to my surprise, the idea was accepted, and a budget and date agreed on, Sunday 6th September 2009. We put together a guest list by contacting people who had been guests at our Friday night meetings—Anneke Wills, Nick Briggs, Gary Russell, Ian Fairbairn, Glen McCoy, Cheryl Hall (who was working in the same school as me in Chesterfield); and Derek put us in touch with Colin Baker, who agreed to be our headliner.

That first Whooverville was a moderate success, with some 70 attendees arriving at Butterley Station, to be brought to the convention in the engine shed at the Swanwick end of the line by steam train. However, we felt we had achieved something, and the feedback was great. The following year, word of mouth was working in our favor and we topped 100 attendees. However, it was clear that a steam railway, in the middle of nowhere on a Sunday was far from the ideal location. We needed an alternative venue.

By this time, the brilliant new QUAD arts center, right in the middle of Derby had opened, so we talked to our contact there, Adam Marsh, and agreed a similar deal with him to that we had had at the railway. As far as I know, this is a unique arrangement among *Doctor Who* conventions. The Whoovers group is effectively paid by QUAD to provide a convention. QUAD sells the tickets and keeps the takings; we choose and book the guests and don't aim to make a profit. This way, we get our convention without having to risk our own money. Numbers have risen steadily over the years and Whooverville now regularly sells over 200 tickets—our capacity is 260.

How did you come to call yourselves "Whoovers"?

There have been a number of *Doctor Who* groups in and around Derby since the 1980, each with a different name and each of which lasted a few years before fading. One of the longest lasting was Whotopia. By 1999, there hadn't been a group for a few years, but members of previous groups had kept in touch. They felt the time was right to start another group and the name Whoovers was chosen—it probably sounded like a good idea at the time and someone probably had the idea for the group logo, based on the Hoover one. It also allowed for a number of vacuum cleaner based jokes; for example, the group newsletter, which ran for a year or two in the early days, was called Vacuum Pack. The chaps involved then liked these puns, we used to have an annual day-out called a Wholiday as well as a garden party called a Zarbicue. I want to stress that I wasn't involved in those days. This November is our 20th anniversary as a group.

For the person who has never attended comic con, can you describe what your convention is like?

Well, Whooverville isn't anything at all like a comic con. It is a traditional convention, like fan-run conventions in the early days used to be. A comic-con is more like an autograph fair, where attendees pay relatively little to get in, but have to pay on top for everything after that—especially autographs, which can be very expensive. We charge a little more to get in but guarantee at least one free autograph for each attendee from every one of our official guests. There are no special tickets to allow people to buy special treatment, queue jumping or anything else. We are a relatively small event with a reputation for running a friendly and relaxed day. We are very proud of that.

We run a program of on-stage interview panels all day, which is the main focus of events. QUAD is a cinema and arts complex and our main hall is the main cinema—The Sir John Hurt Cinema—probably the most comfortable cinema you will ever find. Then we have our autograph room and professionally run photo studio, plus two well stocked dealers and traders' rooms, where you can pick up all sorts of curiosities and bargains.

Any tips or advice for the first-time convention attendee?

Just relax and have fun. We are a fairly small event, so you won't get lost. Work out which autographs and photos you want and which panels you absolutely don't want to miss and plan accordingly. Our experienced and friendly volunteers are there to help and you will find yourself getting into conversations with fellow fans—many of whom have been coming to Whooverville right since the start, so there is always someone to ask if aren't sure about something.

How do you determine which guests to invite to your convention?

Well, we are of course constrained by our budget from QUAD, so we have to work within—or at least not far outside—that. We try to achieve a mix of modern and classic series people, old favorites and new faces, actors and production staff. We try and get at least one or two 'big names' each year—which tends to be classic series Doctors or companions or Modern Series high-profile single episode guest stars or recurring characters. For example, this year at Whooverville 12 our principal guests were Sarah Sutton, Ingrid Oliver, Sophia Myles, Christopher Ryan and the writer Stephen Gallagher.

What makes your convention different from others?

We have been described as the UK's biggest little *Doctor Who* convention, which I like. We are a small event, but we have been lucky to get great guests. We are not here to make money; we are a fan group whose aim is to put on a good event. Of course, QUAD needs to have a good day financially, but that depends on ticket sales and bar takings, not on autograph sales and so on.

What are your thoughts on the struggles of *Doctor Who* Conventions?

Where there have been problems, it seems to me that they have come about for a number of reasons. In some cases, it has come about because an event has attempted to appeal beyond *The Doctor Who* fandom community, by including guests from other shows. On the whole, I suspect that *Doctor Who* fans are less interested in the stars of other shows and equally the fans of those shows are not interested in coming to a *Doctor Who* event. Some events have tried to be too ambitious, too soon. Unless a new event is very prepared to be largely unsuccessful at first and then to grow, it will probably fail. Attempting to emulate the big comic-con style events and booking expensive guests, without the financial clout that these shows have is disastrous. New event organizers—especially fans—need to understand that the guests you invite don't do it for fun; they are there to make money—it's their job. Since 2013, the fees that many guests have been asking has rocketed. The Modern Series big names can command astronomical fees, and this has trickled down in part to those who are less "big names." Then there is the arrival on the scene of the "convention booker," a go-between between the organizer and potential guests. A very small number of these provide a good service and can be helpful. Others do little that the organizers themselves couldn't do. Of course, the booker has to be paid at some point along the line, usually out of increased guests' fees.

As a fan-based show, what particular problems have you encountered trying to put your show together?

Not too many. We have been lucky. When we started, we always said that we would always offer unlimited free autographs for our attendees. Sadly, things have changed and these days our guests expect to be able to charge for autographs, selfies etc. Two years ago, we decided that we had to allow that, on the condition that one free autograph is always given. That is an absolutely unbreakable promise that we make to our attendees. When it comes down to it, we won't invite a guest who is not prepared to agree to that.

A bigger problem is the proliferation of *Doctor Who* events. This year, there was another event on the same day as ours and another a week later, both within 50 miles of Derby. Our event has always been on the Saturday after the August Bank Holiday Monday, but another event, returning after a long gap, has already been announced for that weekend next year. We could have stamped our feet and refused to budge, but that wouldn't have helped anyone, so we have moved Whooverville 12 to late October for 2020. We are lucky that our regular attendees are immensely loyal, so we have every hope that they will come with us.

Do you have a favorite memory from any of your conventions and what was it?

They are mostly concerned with our Whoovers guest meetings, rather than Whooverville. Meeting Terrance Dicks on a number of occasions was an enormous privilege as was interviewing Barry Letts, at one of the last *Doctor Who* events that he attended. There are a number of special interviews that I have been lucky enough to do; Katy Manning, whose head somehow ended up in my lap; Graeme Harper—my memory is that all I said was "So, Graeme," and two hours later, he was still speaking—and being fascinating; and so many more.

The Saturday afternoon meeting with Sylvester was extraordinary. When he was in Derby to launch the panto for the press, at the end of the summer of 2009, we provided a Dalek. I set a bit of an ambush and sent two of our most appealing and (frankly) cute child members to ask Sylvester to agree to do a meeting with us. How could he refuse? We swapped phone numbers and agreed that, although he would be very busy, if a free afternoon or evening came up, he would give me a call. And so, in early December on a Tuesday morning, I was at work (teacher) had just dismissed my period one class and was preparing for period two, when my phone rang (it should by rights have been turned off). It was Sylvester, he was free that Saturday afternoon, could we use him? Of course, we could. I rang Robbie Langton and he booked a room (for once it had to be a pub). We started putting the word out and in four days managed to put together a very successful event, with over 50 attendees. Sylvester was clearly tired but was in sparkling form.

We were delighted and very proud when we were asked to organize the return of Big Finish Day and to bring it to QUAD. We've done two of those now—both sold out and are in the process of organizing the next one for June 2020. The fact that we were trusted to do that was a great tribute to Whooverville.

Who is your favorite guest that has attended your convention?
There have been so many wonderful guests. Terrance of course and having William Russell and Carole-Ann Ford at Whooverville 9 was terrific. I was in awe of David Warner, who came to Whooverville X, but I had to hide it as he is a very shy and humble man and hates to be made a fuss of—but he's DAVID WARNER!

If money wasn't a factor, who is your ideal guest you'd want to invite that you haven't yet?

That's actually quite difficult. Of course, I wouldn't say no to Christopher Eccleston, David Tennant, Matt Smith, Peter Capaldi or Jodie Whittaker, but I actually would worry that having such a prominent guest would change the nature of our event in some way. They might overshadow the event. I think I am going to say Russell T. Davies. Of course, he is a very big name himself, but I think we could cope with him.

What's the most unusual experience that ever happened at one of your conventions?

What made our up minds to move our event after Whooverville 2 was a number of problems that we had at that second convention. The Midland Railway was and is a beautiful site and the volunteers were lovely and had a real passion for what they were doing, but there were difficulties. It seemed as if everyone there belonged to one faction or another, each of which hated all the others. Volunteers at one end of the line had no time for those at the other. Steam people hated diesel people and they all looked down on the narrow-gauge people. We arrived to set up the day before the convention to find a diesel locomotive in the engine shed, being spray-painted:

"But", we inquired, half joking, "It'll be gone by tomorrow—you promised us the shed to ourselves."

"No, they're painting it in here, all weekend."

Those who attended Whooverville 2 will still remember the fumes from the spray paint; some came close to passing out.

How can people find out more about your convention?

The easiest place is on Facebook—either at the Whoovers Group or on the Whooverville event page (or the Big Finish Day one). They can follow us on Twitter @Whoovers and there's also a website at www.whooverville.org

Krystal Moore: The Doctor from *Doctor Who Velocity*

Congratulations to you and *Doctor Who Velocity* for reaching 1.4k subscribers and over 61,000 views on YouTube. Did you ever imagine your short fan-film series would take off like it did?

I speak for everyone who was involved when I say that we are over the moon with the response. Between all our pages we have something like 270K views... That's like the whole city I live in! We made the first episode hoping it would do well, but we hadn't planned on making a full series... then the first episode got enough interest that we thought we would make a few more and even try our hand at some audio dramas... all of which have done better than we could have imagined. I mean, we got Sophie Aldred involved in the 4th one, which I couldn't have dreamed possible... so we're probably going to continue making them for the foreseeable future. The great thing about *The Doctor Who* concept is that it is so flexible, we've now established a great vehicle for whatever short films we'd like to create. You can take any story idea and usually add The Doctor somehow to give it a sci-fi twist.

Can you tell me a little bit about your acting background?

I've always been theatrical. As a child I used the neighborhood to put on plays, puppet shows, etc. I was Drama Club President in High School, and then worked with the local small theater for a few years in a variety of roles on stage and off. I came to the "city," and by that, I mean everywhere in Idaho is rural except the capital, the "city," Haha! I was quick to get involved in performance groups and even started doing stand-up comedy. I got to meet so many talented people in media, production, and performance. Of course, I had to use all this talent to weave my own stories, and *Doctor Who* had long been a favorite of mine.

I understand from speaking with you previously on *The Legend of the Traveling TARDIS Radio Show*, you had already been discussing about creating this fan-film series during Matt Smith's run as The Doctor.

Yes. Initially, the idea was a parody, like a sketch comedy, of The Doctor as a woman... I guess I could feel it on the horizon. About this time, I had my second child, so that delayed the production of this idea, and I'm glad that it did. When Capaldi announced he was leaving, I just knew it was time. To be honest, I didn't think the BBC would actually cast a woman quite yet. I was thrilled when they did, it told me we were on to something. At that point the whole concept really began to take form, it morphed into something a bit more Who-ey in nature, not outright a parody, but not leaving off my love for laughter. *Doctor Who* hits that fantastical place between sci-fi and fantasy; where things are outrageous, but you accept them, the dialogue is silly and philosophical, the characters are out of this world but deeply human.

How would you describe your Doctor?

I think each actor that portrays *Doctor Who* brings a little bit of themselves to the character, while using The Doctors who came before as a jumping off point. I'm a powerful woman, a nurturing mother, and a silly goose. I like to think that I infuse my Doctor with those three things. Sexy, smart, and silly.

I absolutely love your sonic screwdriver! What inspired its creation?

Budget constraints and creativity. I use what I have in life, and I think that's a very 'Doctor' thing about me, ingenuitive. What I had was craft supplies and LEGOs, so I kept putting them together in ways until I had created one that I liked. I'm very pleased with how it turned out. I like the sleek look of it, reminiscent of the first sonics.

I have got to admit, my favorite part of your costume is your hat lol! How did you come up with the concept?

Thanks! I love the hat. To be honest, we don't spend too much time on design, but then my partner and I are both well versed in it and have working experience, so we can pull that part together pretty quickly. It's not the place to spend too much time on a small project, and a fan film is a small project. Our objective is to produce a solid story with relatable characters, because that is what carries the whole thing. With that in mind, a lot of the costume elements are out of my closet, though I did buy the hat for this… I don't know why but I just knew she had a bowler for some reason. I went to the mall to find one and lucked out at the first stop in H&M. The feathers, however, were from my craft supplies.

(Maybe this isn't for you) Is it at all weird to act out your own script you've written?

Writing and acting are quite separate processes so to act it well, you have to forget that whole writing process and focus on living in the circumstance and not worrying about what is coming next, or what the 'meaning' is. A writer can see the whole world, but the character only has their drive and perspective so it's important to try and forget all the other details that don't matter from their perspective. It's a lot of compartmentalizing… but a great deal of acting is brainwashing yourself to believe in the situation you are in, believe in the person you are, and have the memories of this character. It's weirder from the writer's perspective than the actors. I have to give myself permission to write cool lines for me to say, and the writer brain is very self-critical, so that's the part that is a challenge in letting myself go all the way in writing the character. Once I put on the actor brain and start forgetting everything I don't need to know and planting those character memories, then it is easy and not weird at all… because, I'm The Doctor.

What's the typical time frame from script to finished product for an episode?

Scripts can take a couple of months to think about in our spare time, and then maybe a month to write.

We make notes and get the structure very firm before we write. The writing of the actual script is usually the last process—we've already got the story structure down and planned what happens on each page. There's this weird myth about writers block you hear about—people staring at a blank page. We've both worked in professional marketing and entertainment settings where that doesn't happen. You decide on a purpose, theme and duration and then you plan it out. Then you write out what you planned. Of course, some days you are more inspired than others, but the objective is always to finish it and make it entertaining.

Is there anything you'd like to explore with your Doctor on *Doctor Who Velocity* that you haven't yet?

Yes, many, many things! The great thing about *Doctor Who* is that it is so flexible, and each show can be a different genre or subject. With each episode we try and add an extra element that perhaps the BBC would not address—although when you look at how many episodes, books and audio adventures there are—you can always find someone who's made something similar! We thought our recent episode 4 with Ace and the rave scene was original, only to find there was a very similar Big Finish audio adventure called The Rapture!

How incredible you were able to get Sophie Aldred, who played the Seventh Doctor's companion, Ace, involved in the last episode. Were you surprised when she and her agent said yes to your inquiry?

For our fourth episode we really wanted to step up the production on our show and try some new things. We made contacts with some local people who had cinema quality cameras and we decided to rely a little less on green screen effects and try and film most of it in-camera. Then we were trying to think, "what would be a great surprise or twist" and since we'd written the show in 1989, we thought, "oh Ace would totally be into this dance scene!" We toyed with making our own version of Ace, and having a local actress play our version of Ace, but we just loved the idea of bringing Sophie back somehow.

As we'd added the Pirate Radio element, we released that we could get Sophie to record some audio and fit that into a phone call. It still seemed like a crazy idea that couldn't happen—but we thought there was no harm in trying. We put together a little presentation of our show, with a request and the script, and sent it over to her agent.

We got an email back a couple of days later saying Sophie had agreed to do it! We were over the moon!

Are you able to tease the readers of this book a little bit about your upcoming Christmas audiobook or episode?

The next Christmas audio adventure will be the third one with our audio companion DJ Lloyd. Lloyd is actually a real person—he's an antiques dealer and local DJ in the East of England who always has a bunch of hilarious stories on his Facebook page—an old friend of ours. So, when we started making our audio adventures, we thought he would be an amusing character. This will be the third time using his character, so we thought we'd create something a bit more epic to round off the DJ Lloyd trilogy. The

Master will be coming back and he sucks The Doctor and DJ Lloyd into an adventure that involves them meeting many real historical heroes from British history. It's going to be a fun adventure.

Are there any other acting projects you are currently involved in?

The rest of my performance creativity and energy goes entirely into comedy. I love stand-up like few other things in life. It is this incredible balance between being 100% authentically yourself and also 100% authentically this character you create. I produce a couple different comedy shows also with niche audiences. One could check that out on my website… where they will also find an interview with me on NPR about one of these shows… which was such a dream come true. Good grief, I am such a Public Radio Nerd. That's where you're gonna see me fan-girling hard.

How can people find out more about you and *Doctor Who Velocity?*

We have plenty of social media:

www.facebook.com/doctorwhovelocity
www.instagram.com/doctorwhovelocity/
www.Twitter.com/drwhovelocity
www.youtube.com/doctorwhovelocity
https://thekrystalmoore.com/
www.chrisphillips.tv

David Solomons:
Author of Doctor Who: The Secret in Vault 13

How long have you been writing?

I wasn't one of those kids that wrote endless short stories. I wish I had been. Instead, my first experience of creative writing was a collaborative effort at primary school, aged nine or 10, when our class co-wrote an original play, which we performed at the end of term. I caught the writing bug then, but it was many years before what I would describe as my official starting-point. That happened when in my 20's a friend bought me William Goldman's book *Adventures in the Screen Trade*. It was the first time I'd seen a screenplay and I decided to have a go at writing my own. I wrote five screenplays that summer and, amazingly, one of them led to me getting a film agent. That was 25 years ago.

Seeing that your book debuted only a few months after the new show first aired, did you get any inside tips from the show or the publisher on how to go about writing the 13th Doctor and her companions?

There was a great deal of secrecy surrounding that first season and it was a struggle to get much information out of anyone about the new show. I based my take on 13 on the one word she spoke after her regeneration, 'Brilliant!' and I took an educated guess at the rest. As the novel went through various revisions, more information was forthcoming, so I could fill in the blanks and adjust some of the dialogue. The one thing I needed, but didn't have until the last moment, was an image of the TARDIS interior. Thankfully, a visual arrived in my inbox just in time, with strict instructions to destroy the file as soon as I was done with it. No leaks from me!

Where did the concept for this novel come from?

I recalled reading about the Global Seed Vault in the Arctic Circle, a repository for seeds from across Earth, held securely in a vault under a mountain so that in the event of a natural disaster or some other catastrophe that wipes out the crop, the land can be reseeded. I thought that it sounded remarkable, and then I saw a photo of the place and it looks straight out of a science-fiction story. I began to speculate about the existence of a Galactic Seed Vault that contained seeds from across the universe, and something very dangerous in the vault at its heart.

Speaking with other friends who work in various areas of *Doctor Who*, did the publisher or show approach you or did you approach them?

This was one of those rare occasions when I didn't have to go in and pitch my heart out and then endure an agonizing wait for a phone call. The publisher came to me, mainly because I've written a series of novels for children (*My Brother is a Superhero* is the first in that series). They wanted a child-friendly *Doctor Who* story for the same age group that enjoys my superhero stories.

How much time did you spend on research for this book?

Time, appropriately enough, was the one thing I did not have while writing this book. In fact, I almost turned down the opportunity to write it because I thought I couldn't deliver the first draft in the time frame required. But how could I say no to The Doctor?! I had 12 weeks to write the story from a standing start. I researched as I went, filling in blanks using my sketchy knowledge of the world, the many online resources that ardent *Doctor Who* fans have created, and the brains of my editor, Emil, who is a fount of knowledge when it comes to *Who*, *Star Wars*, etc.

What challenges did you find when you were writing this book?

As I've said, the time frame was the biggest. Beyond that, there was the challenge of creating a new alien civilization before breakfast every day. At least it sometimes felt like that. I decided to write the book in an episodic fashion, partly to echo the format of original *Who* that I had enjoyed as a child, but mostly because I knew that if necessary I could rewrite a section without affecting every part of the novel, or even replace a section with something entirely new. Given the tight deadline, this seemed like a good plan, and it did in fact work out as predicted. I had to revise one part quite heavily, thanks to an editorial note. It was one of those notes that when you read it you know that one: it is brilliant and right. And two it's going to cause you a lot of work but will be worth it in the end.

Mackenzie Flohr

What was your favorite part of the book to write and why?

Doctor Who was a huge part of my childhood, so at this point in my career to be given the opportunity to play in that world was a wondrous thing. I had to pinch myself every time I sat down to work. All of which is to say I loved writing every part of the book. Although, I'm particularly fond of the section set in what appears to be an unassuming London garden.

I recently learned your audiobook was read by Sophie Aldred, who played my favorite Classic companion, Ace. How did that come about?

Isn't she brilliant? Absolutely nothing to do with me, though. As much as I'd like to claim responsibility for such an excellent piece of casting.

Have you met any of the current cast or crew on _Doctor Who_? If not, who would you like to meet?

I haven't met any of the current cast or crew, but I did work with Karen Gillan a few years ago—she, of course, played legendary companion Amy Pond. I wrote a low-budget feature film, which she starred in, playing the role of an author with writer's block. As for the current series, as much as I'd like to meet any of the actors, I think I'd love it even more if I could see the TARDIS up close.

What advice would you give for someone who really wants to write for _Doctor Who_?

Be ready. Have a great story idea, one that you've worked through from beginning to end. Ideally, one you can pitch in thirty seconds. You never know when you might find yourself stuck in a lift with the *Doctor Who* commissioning editor!

I understand readers will be getting the opportunity to see you writing more *Doctor Who* books for Jodie's Doctor in 2020. Can you share anything about your upcoming book, *Doctor Who: The Maze of Doom*?

The first one was galaxy-hopping, this one's more Earth-bound. A lot of action involving ancient clockwork Minotaurs, robot attack dogs, submarines, cable cars and undersea bases. I'd go so far as to say there's a James Bond flavor to this one.

Which other books that you've written would you recommend to readers wanting to learn more about you?

I've written five books in the "My Brother is a Superhero" series, about an embittered younger brother who missed out on superpowers because he needed to go for a wee. They're funny, fast-paced and full of references that fans of *Doctor Who* might recognize.

How can people find out more about you?

I'm very mysterious. Either that, or just lazy about updating my website david-solomons.com

Alisa Stern: Creator of Doctor Puppet

I want to thank Alisa Stern for taking time out of her very busy schedule to answer some questions for me. What inspired you to create Doctor Puppet?

No problem! Back in 2012, I was teaching a stop motion animation class and needed to make an example puppet for the students. Matt Smith was The Doctor at the time, and I thought his physical appearance really lent itself to puppet design, and so I made him into one. I wanted to share the puppet with people outside the class, so I started a Tumblr blog for puppet photos. Eventually, this led to the YouTube channel and the fully animated episodes. So, you could say that my love of *Doctor Who* and stop motion animation together inspired it.

Did you ever imagine it taking off like it did on YouTube?

I was more surprised when it took off on Tumblr originally! The popularity there is what pushed me to invest more time and commit to making more puppets and a full story. It was a lot of work, so the early success of the channel is what kept me and the rest of the team going.

What was the typical time frame from script to finished product for an episode?

It depends on how complicated the episode is and how much time the team and I have to devote to it. The quickest turnaround was "A Timelord Christmas" because Erin (animator/story boarder) and I had just become unemployed at the same time. We made that entire episode in about six weeks because we were working on it full time. "The Twelfth Planet" took over two years to make because it's the longest episode and features the most puppets and sets.

What kind of challenges did you face?

Ironically… mainly time and space! Everyone who worked on Doctor Puppet has other jobs—jobs that pay better money too. So, Doctor Puppet was a nights and weekends passion project mainly. Space was another massive challenge. I live in New York City and have a very small one-bedroom apartment. I made Doctor Puppet in my living room, so I sacrificed almost all my space for those puppets.

I noticed you are going to be a guest at SD Who Con which is, ironically, also being interviewed for this book. For someone who hasn't seen your show in person before, will it be similar to what you have on your YouTube channel?

When I do panels at cons, I tend to screen all the episodes and then do a Q&A. So, that part is just like watching it on YouTube, only the puppets and I are in the room with you! I think it's even more special for me because I get to watch people watch Doctor Puppet, which I hardly ever get to do.

How difficult is it to travel with all of your puppets? I think I'd be a nerve wreck thinking they would get damaged or lost by the airline!

It is difficult and nerve-racking, but I've done it a few times now, so I don't worry as much. When I fly, the puppets end up taking up all the space in my carry-on luggage. I wrap each one in bubble wrap, so they have a safe trip. I always bring a little repair kit in case something needs fixing. The puppets constantly break anyway, so I wouldn't be too shocked if a little accident happened.

I recently read that you were featured in *The Doctor Who* documentary, *Doctor Who: Earth Conquest.* How did that opportunity come about?

That was back in 2014! A producer working on the documentary found out about me somehow and sent me an email just a few days before the World Tour was arriving in New York City. We met in Madison Square Park for a quick interview. Afterwards, she mentioned that there was a chance the documentary crew could get some original audio we could animate the puppets to.

Since Peter Capaldi and Jenna Coleman actually contributed their voice talents to the documentary, have you been able to speak to either of them about Doctor Puppet?

And yes, Peter and Jenna were able to record that audio for us! We never met them, but I was told that Peter was excited to voice his puppet.

Have you had any strange Doctor Puppet fan encounters? If so, what was it?

Oh yes—many! My all-time favorite is when a grown man in full Batman cosplay spotted me at New York Comic Con with a puppet. He did a double take, then ran over and fan-girled all over us. It was hilarious. Also, someone once thought I was cosplaying as myself. He didn't believe I was the actual creator of Doctor Puppet holding a real puppet from it.

One of my favorite moments is getting to see your Jodie Whittaker puppet featured on the cover of the 13th Doctor comics. Can you share with my readers, how that came about?

That's one of my favorites, too! I met the Titan Comics brand manager at Gallifrey One in 2018. I was bold enough to ask him if I could contribute to the comics, and it just so happened there was a perfect opportunity for me on the horizon. The lesson is never be afraid to ask!

Last time I had spoken with you, you were working on a new animation series, which wasn't *Doctor Who* related. How is that project going so far?

It's going very well! And it's not actually a new series—it's just a one off-short film called *Sum of Its Parts*. It's stop motion animated, but it's very different from Doctor Puppet. I'm using a different stop motion technique and I'm animating outside instead of on a set. It's been very different and fun to make.

Any future plans on possibly seeing Doctor Puppet back on Indiegogo for a Jodie puppet series?

No plans for that now!

How can people find out more about you and Doctor Puppet?

Check out my YouTube channel where you can watch all The Doctor Puppet episodes as well as lots of behind the scenes content. You can also follow me on Twitter, Instagram, Facebook, and Tumblr.

youtube.com/HelloDoctorPuppet
Twitter: @TheDoctorPuppet
Instagram: @DoctorPuppet
doctorpuppet.tumblr.com
facebook.com/thedoctorpuppet

Appendices

"I'll be fine, in the end, hopefully. Well, I have to be, because you guys need help, and if there's one thing I'm certain of, when people need help, I never refuse. Right? This is gonna be fun."
-13th Doctor

While you are waiting for Series 12 to premiere on television, here are some additional venues where you can continue following the 13th Doctor and her companions as they travel across the universe in the TARDIS. Plus, enjoy some additional exclusive interviews with some of the people who have contributed their talents and time towards continuing on The Doctor's message.

Right! Let's get a shift on!

Appendix A: Doctor Who Annuals

Doctor Who: Official Annual 2019

By BBC

The Doctor Who Annual 2019 will be an incredible insight into the 13th Doctor and her first journey in time and space. There will be an all-new TARDIS to explore, alien tech to examine (with a brand-new sonic screwdriver) and monsters to defeat.

You'll learn all about The Doctor's friends, and have their help along the way, as you solve puzzles, examine fact files on The Doctor's enemies, and read exciting comic strips and stories. There will be exclusive secrets from the last series, and a look ahead at what's to come for the Thirteenth Doctor.

A must-read for all *Doctor Who* fans, old and new.

Series: Doctor Who
Hardcover: 64 pages
Publisher: Penguin Group UK
Date: November 13, 2018
Language: English
ISBN-10: 1405933763
ISBN-13: 978-1405933766

Doctor Who: Official Annual 2020
By BBC Children's Books, Penguin Random House

The universe is calling . . .

Join The Doctor for another adventure in the TARDIS alongside her friends Yasmin, Ryan and Graham! This amazing annual is packed with stories, puzzles, games and amazing facts about The Doctor's travels, triumphs and enemies.

Series: Doctor Who
Hardcover: 64 pages
Publisher: Penguin Group UK
Date: October 1, 2019
Language: English
ISBN-10: 1405940859
ISBN-13: 978-1405940856

Appendix B: 13th Doctor Novels

Doctor Who: The Good Doctor
By Juno Dawson

For a Good Doctor there's only one rule: first do no harm.

On the planet of Lobos, The Doctor halts a violent war between the native Loba and human colonists.

Job done; the TARDIS crew departs—only for Ryan to discover he's left his phone behind. Again. Upon returning, The Doctor finds that the TARDIS has slipped hundreds of years into the future—and that something has gone badly wrong.

The Loba are now slaves, serving human zealots who worship a godlike figure known as The Good Doctor. It's time for The Doctor to face up to the consequences of her last visit. With Lobos on the brink of catastrophe, will she be able to make things, right?

Featuring the Thirteenth Doctor, Yasmin, Ryan and Graham, as played by Jodie Whittaker, Mandip Gill, Tosin Cole and Bradley Walsh.

Series: Doctor Who
Hardcover: 256 pages
Publisher: Penguin Group UK
Date: November 13, 2018
Language: English
ISBN-10: 1785943847
ISBN-13: 978-1785943843

Doctor Who: Combat Magicks
By Steve Cole

How do you win a battle when the dead fight on?

The TARDIS arrives in Gaul in 451AD, on the eve of battle between the forces of Attila the Hun and those of the crumbling Roman Empire. But The Doctor soon finds that sinister, supernatural creatures are helping both sides.

While Graham makes allies in the Roman camp and Ryan is pursued by the enigmatic Legion of Smoke, The Doctor and Yasmin are pressed into service as Attila's personal sorcerers. But The Doctor knows there is science behind the combat magicks—and that the true war will pit all humanity against a ruthless alien threat.

Featuring the Thirteenth Doctor, Yasmin, Ryan and Graham, as played by Jodie Whittaker, Mandip Gill, Tosin Cole and Bradley Walsh.

Series: Doctor Who
Hardcover: 256 pages
Publisher: Penguin Group UK
Date: December 4, 2018
Language: English
ISBN-10: 1785943693
ISBN-13: 978-1785943690

Doctor Who: Molten Heart
By Una McCormack

Don't dig too deep. You never know what you'll find beneath the surface.

Deep below the surface of the planet Adamantine lies a crystalline wonder world of lava seas and volcanic islands, home to living rock-people.

But when The Doctor and her friends arrive on Adamantine, they find it under threat. The seas are shrinking, the magma is cooling, and mysterious, fatal seething pools are spreading fast.

Something has come to Adamantine—but what does it want? Fearing an invasion is underway, The Doctor must lead an expedition to the surface of the world to save its molten heart…

Featuring the Thirteenth Doctor, Yasmin, Ryan and Graham, as played by Jodie Whittaker, Mandip Gill, Tosin Cole and Bradley Walsh.

Series: Doctor Who
Hardcover: 256 pages
Publisher: Penguin Group UK
Date: November 20, 2018
Language: English
ISBN-10: 1785943634
ISBN-13: 978-1785943638

Doctor Who: Star Tales

By Steve Cole, Paul Magrs, Jenny T Colgan, Jo
Cotterill, Trevor Baxendale, Mike Tucker

*'Even though they're gone from the world, they're never
gone from me.'*

The Doctor is many things—curious, funny, brave,
protective of her friends...and a shameless name dropper.
While she and her companions battled aliens and traveled
across the universe, The Doctor hinted at a host of
previous, untold adventures with the great and the good:
we discovered she got her sunglasses from Pythagoras (or
was it Audrey Hepburn?); lent a mobile phone to Elvis;
had an encounter with Amelia Earhart where she
discovered that a pencil-thick spider web can stop a
plane; had a 'wet weekend' with Harry Houdini, learning
how to escape from chains underwater; and more.

In this collection of new stories, *Star Tales* takes
you on a rip-roaring ride through history, from 500 BC
to the swinging 60's, going deeper into The Doctor's
notorious name-dropping and revealing the truth
behind these anecdotes.

Series: Doctor Who
Hardcover: 256 pages   **Language:** English
Publisher: Penguin Group UK   **ISBN-10:** 1785944711
Date: December 17, 2019   **ISBN-13:** 978-1785944710

Doctor Who: The Women Who Lived True Tales of: Brilliant Women from across Time & Space

By Christel Dee & Simon Guerrier

Meet the women who run the Whoniverse

From Sarah Jane Smith to Bill Potts, from Susan Foreman to the Thirteenth Doctor, women are the beating heart of *Doctor Who*. Whether they're facing down Daleks or thwarting a Nestene invasion, these women don't hang around waiting to be rescued—they roll their sleeves up and get stuck in. Scientists and soldiers, queens and canteen workers, they don't let anything hold them back.

Featuring historical women such as Agatha Christie and Queen Victoria alongside fan favorites like Rose Tyler and Missy, The Women Who Lived tells the stories of women throughout space and time. Beautifully illustrated by a team of all-female artists, this collection of inspirational tales celebrates the power of women to change the universe.

Series: Doctor Who
Hardcover: 224 pages
Publisher: Penguin Group UK
Date: November 20, 2018
Language: English
ISBN-10: 1785943596
ISBN-13: 978-1785943591

Doctor Who: Thirteen Doctors 13 Stories

By Naomi Alderman, Malorie Blackman, Holly Black,
Neil Gaiman, Derek Landy, Charlie Higson, Alex
Scarrow, Richelle Mead, Patrick Ness, Philip Reeve,
Marcus Sedgwick, Michael Scott, Eoin Colfer

*A new version of this much-loved anthology, with a
brand-new story featuring the brand-new Thirteenth
Doctor from literary sensation Naomi Alderman!*

Twelve wonderful tales of adventure, science, magic,
monsters and time travel—featuring all twelve
Doctors—are waiting for you in this very special *Doctor
Who* book.

And now they're joined by a very exciting, and very
exclusive, new tale—written by Naomi Alderman,
author of *The Power*—that will star the Thirteenth
Doctor, as she battles to save the universe with her three
close and trusted friends.

Other authors featured are: Eoin Colfer, Michael
Scott, Marcus Sedgwick, Philip Reeve, Patrick Ness,
Richelle Mead, Malorie Blackman, Alex Scarrow, Charlie
Higson, Derek Landy, Neil Gaiman, and Holly Black.

Series: Doctor Who
Paperback: 624 pages   **Language:** English
Publisher: Penguin Group UK   **ISBN-10:** 0241356172
Date: March 26, 2019   **ISBN-13:** 978-0241356173

Doctor Who: The Target Storybook

By Terrance Dicks, Matthew Sweet, Simon Guerrier, Colin Baker, Matthew Waterhouse, Jenny T Colgan, Jacqueline Rayner, Una McCormack, Steve Cole, Vinay Patel, George Mann, Susie Day, Mike Tucker, Joy Wilkinson, Beverly Sanford

We're all stories in the end...

In this exciting collection you'll find all-new stories spinning off from some of your favorite *Doctor Who* moments across the history of the series. Learn what happened next, what went on before, and what occurred off-screen in an inventive selection of sequels, side-trips, foreshadowing and first-hand accounts—and look forward too, with a brand-new adventure for the Thirteenth Doctor.

Each story expands in thrilling ways upon aspects of *Doctor Who*'s enduring legend. With contributions from show luminaries past and present—including Colin Baker, Matthew Waterhouse, Vinay Patel, Joy Wilkinson and Terrance Dicks—*The Target Storybook* is a once-in-a-lifetime tour around the wonders of the Whoniverse.

Series: Doctor Who
Hardcover: 256 pages   **Language:** English
Publisher: Penguin Group UK   **ISBN-10:** 1785943847
Date: November 13, 2018   **ISBN-13:** 978-1785943843

Doctor Who: The 13 Doctors
By Adam Hargreaves

The greatest mash-up in the entire Whoniverse is here! Join all 13 Doctors—from Dr. First to the brand-new 13th Doctor—on an amazing adventure through time and space, written and illustrated by Adam Hargreaves. This brilliant slipcase contains 13 individual paperbacks.

Series: Doctor Who / Roger Hargreaves
Paperback: 416 pages
Publisher: BBC Children's Books
Date: March 7, 2019
Language: English
ISBN-10: 1405933836
ISBN-13: 978-1405933834

Doctor Who: Dr. Thirteenth
By Adam Hargreaves

An all-new *Doctor Who* adventure featuring the Thirteenth—and first female!—Doctor re-imagined in the style of Roger Hargreaves.

The Doctor, Graham, and Ryan try and come up with a fabulous surprise for Yaz on her birthday. And what an explosive surprise it is

Series: Doctor Who / Roger Hargreaves
Paperback: 32 pages
Publisher: Penguin Young Readers
Date: January 8, 2019
Language: English
ISBN-10: 1524788600
ISBN-13: 978-1524788605

Doctor Who: The Secret in Vault 13
By David Solomons

A sinister school where graduation means death...

A monstrous mystery lurking below a quiet London street…

A desperate plea for help delivered by... hang on, a potted plant?

The Doctor has been summoned. The galaxy is in terrible danger, and only a Time Lord can save it. But to do so, she must break into an ancient vault on a remote and frozen world—from which nobody has ever returned alive...

Can The Doctor and her friends Yaz, Ryan and Graham uncover the shocking secret in Vault 13?

Series: Doctor Who
Hardcover: 304 pages
Publisher: Random House Books for Young Readers
Date: November 6, 2018
Language: English
ISBN-10: 1984895982
ISBN-13: 978-1984895981

Doctor Who: The Maze of Doom
By David Solomons

An ancient artifact buried deep within the TARDIS leads The Doctor back to London, where a deadly predator prowls the tunnels beneath the city. As the Time Lord and her friends investigate, they uncover a mystery that will take them from a secret mountain base to the depths of the ocean - and if they cannot solve it, one of them will perish.

In order to save her friend, The Doctor must solve the riddle of... the Maze of Death!

Series: Doctor Who
Hardcover: 304 pages
Publisher: BBC Children's Books
Date: November 7, 2019
Language: English
ISBN-10: 1405937629
ISBN-13: 978-1405937627

Doctor Who: At Childhood's End
By Sophie Aldred

Past or future, which path do you choose?

Past, present and future collide as the Thirteenth Doctor meets classic Doctor Who companion Ace—in the first epic novel from the woman who played her, Sophie Aldred.

Once, a girl called Ace traveled the universe with the Doctor—until, in the wake of a terrible tragedy they parted company. Decades later, she is known as Dorothy McShane, the reclusive millionaire philanthropist who heads global organization A Charitable Earth.

And Dorothy is haunted by terrible nightmares, vivid dreams that begin just as scores of young runaways are vanishing from the dark alleyways of London. Could the disappearances be linked to sightings of sinister creatures lurking in the city shadows? Why has an alien satellite entered a secret orbit around the Moon?

Investigating the satellite with Ryan, Graham and Yaz, the Doctor is thrown together with Ace once more. Together they must unravel a malevolent plot that will cost thousands of lives. But can the Doctor atone for her past incarnation's behavior—and how much must Ace sacrifice to win victory not only for herself, but the Earth?

Date: April 21, 2020

Series: Doctor Who   **Language:** English
Hardcover: 352 pages   **ISBN-10:** 1785944991
Publisher: Penguin Group UK   **ISBN-13:** 978-1785944994

Doctor Who: The Witchfinders (Target Collection)
By Joy Wilkinson

"I am an expert on witchcraft, Doctor, but I wish to learn more. Before you die, I want answers."

The TARDIS lands in the Lancashire village of Bilehurst Cragg in the 17th century, and the Doctor, Ryan, Graham and Yaz soon become embroiled in a witch trial run by the local landowner. Fear stalks the land, and the arrival of King James I only serves to intensify the witch hunt.

But the Doctor soon realizes there is something more sinister than paranoia and superstition at work. Tendrils of living mud stir in the ground and the dead lurch back to horrifying life as an evil alien presence begins to revive. The Doctor and her friends must save not only the people of Bilehurst Cragg from the wakening forces, but the entire world.

Series: Doctor Who
Hardcover: 208 pages
Publisher: BBC Books
Date: July 23, 2020
Language: English
ISBN-10: 1785945025
ISBN-13: 978-1785945021

Appendix C: 13th Doctor Comics (Titan Comics)

Doctor Who: The Road to The Thirteenth Doctor

By James Peaty, Jody Houser, Rachel Stott, Pasqualo Qualano, Brian Williamson

Join the road to the Thirteenth Doctor with this essential comics collection, featuring three standalone tales of the Tenth, Eleventh and Twelfth Doctors, and a tantalizing pro-logue to the Thirteenth Doctor's All New Comics Adventures!

The Tenth Doctor, Gabby, and Cindy have their work cut out for them when they encounter a lost spaceship... whose crew is being absorbed by mysterious, ghostly creatures! But everything is not as it seems, especially when disturbing facts about the crew come to light!

The Eleventh Doctor and Alice visit 19th Century San Francisco, but there's just one problem—it's full of robots! Do the automata come in peace or does their displacement in time signal something sinister?

The Twelfth Doctor and Bill find London's Piccadilly Circus transformed into an empty wasteland... of pterodactyls!

And on the *Road to the Thirteenth Doctor*, written and drawn by the creative team of the all-new ongoing Thirteenth Doctor series, meet a brand-new character who has been drawn to incarnations of The Doctor all throughout history—but will they be friend or foe?!

Mackenzie Flohr

Series: Doctor Who: The Road to the Thirteenth Doctor
Paperback: 96 pages
Publisher: Titan Comics
Date: December 18, 2018
Language: English
ISBN-10: 1785869310
ISBN-13: 978-1785869310

Doctor Who: The Thirteenth Doctor Volume 0—The Many Lives of Doctor Who (Doctor Who: Thirteenth **Doctor)**
By Richard Dinnick, Giorgia Sposito, Pasquale Qualano

An introduction to the brand-new thirteenth Doctor, featuring multiple stories of previous incarnations of The Doctor.

The ultimate celebration of The Doctor's many, many lives, a perfect beginner's guide and a brilliant tribute for long-term fans to enjoy! It's said that your life flashes before your eyes when you die: as The Doctor regenerates from his Twelfth incarnation to her Thirteenth, she relives memories from her many incarnations, showcasing unseen adventures from EVERY version of The Doctor!

Series: Doctor Who: Thirteenth Doctor
Paperback: 64 pages
Publisher: Titan Comics
Date: October 9, 2018
Language: English
ISBN-10: 1785868721
ISBN-13: 978-1785868726

Doctor Who: The Thirteenth Doctor Volume 1 (Doctor Who The 13th Doctor)
By Jody Houser, Rachael Stott, Roberta Ingranata, Enrica Eren Angiolini

Bestselling comics writer Jody Houser and fan-favorite artist Rachael Stott launch The Doctor into a new universe of unforgettable adventure! Featuring Jodie Whittaker as the first female incarnation of The Doctor!

Bursting straight out of her hit new television adventures, this first collection of the Thirteenth Doctor's comic book tales is a scorchingly fresh incarnation, taking the show—and its comic strip adventures—where no Doctor has gone before!

Facing off against vile villains and misunderstood monsters in flavors both human and alien, The Doctor and her friends must push the limits of time and space, confronting evils deliberate and accidental all throughout history - and uncovering secrets long-hidden and wonders never-seen along the way!

Perfect for fans old and new alike, this is an awe-inspiring jumping on point to The *Doctor Who* comics mythos.

Buy it, read it, then travel back in time to read it for the first time all over again...! Collects *Doctor Who: The Thirteenth Doctor #1-4.*

Series: Doctor Who: The 13th Doctor (Book 1)
Paperback: 112 pages
Publisher: Titan Comics
Date: May 7, 2019
Language: English
ISBN-10: 1785866761
ISBN-13: 978-1785866760

Doctor Who: The Thirteenth Doctor Volume 2

By Jody Houser, Rachael Stott, Roberta Ingranata, Enrica Eren Angiolini

Bestselling comics writer Jody Houser and fan-favorite artist Rachael Stott bring you the second volume of the hit series featuring Jodie Whittaker as the first female incarnation of The Doctor.

Bursting straight out of her hit television adventures, this second collection of the Thirteenth Doctor's comic book tales is a scorchingly fresh incarnation, taking the show—and its comic strip adventures—where no Doctor has gone before!

Facing off against vile villains and misunderstood monsters in flavors both human and alien, The Doctor and her friends must push the limits of time and space, confronting evils deliberate and accidental all throughout history—and uncovering secrets long-hidden and wonders never-seen along the way!

Perfect for fans old and new alike, this is an awe-inspiring jumping on point to The *Doctor Who* comics mythos.

Buy it, read it, then travel back in time to read it for the first time all over again...! Collects *Doctor Who: The Thirteenth Doctor #5-8.*

Series: Doctor Who: The 13th Doctor (Book 2)
Paperback
Publisher: Titan Comics
Date: August 27, 2019
Language: English
ISBN-10: 1785866915
ISBN-13: 978-1785866913

Doctor Who: The Thirteenth Doctor - Old Friends
By Jody Houser, Roberta Ingranata, Enrica Eren Angiolini, Tracy Bailey

Bestselling comics writer Jody Houser continues her critically acclaimed Doctor Who run with another thrilling adventure featuring the 13th Doctor, Graham, Yaz, and Ryan.

Bestselling comics writer Jody Houser and fan-favorite artist Roberta Ingranata bring you the third volume of the hit series featuring Jodie Whittaker as the first female incarnation of The Doctor.

Buy it, read it, then travel back in time to read it for the first time all over again...! Collects *Doctor Who: The Thirteenth Doctor #9-12.*

Series: Doctor Who: The 13th Doctor (Book 3)
Paperback: 112 pages
Publisher: Titan Comics
Date: November 26, 2019
Language: English
ISBN-10: 1785866923
ISBN-13: 978-1785866920

Appendix D: 13th Doctor Video Games

Doctor Who: The Runaway

This past May, *Doctor Who* fans in the UK were able to get their hands on the first virtual reality video game in the franchise, which was written by Victoria Asare-Archer, called *Doctor Who: The Runaway*. Segun Akinola, musical composer for Series 11, also returned with brand new music composed for this game.

In this animated virtual reality game, the 13th Doctor, voiced by Jodie Whittaker, recruits you, the player, as her new companion. You are given a sonic screwdriver and are tasked with helping The Doctor return a dangerous creature called Volta to his home planet. She even lets you steer the TARDIS!

Zillah Watson, head of BBC VR Hub, which was one of the producers of the game, said in a BBC press release, "This is the most ambitious project yet from our team in the BBC VR Hub, and the result is a magical adventure that *Doctor Who* fans everywhere will simply love. It also shows the enormous potential that virtual reality has for creating new kinds of experiences that appeal to mainstream audiences."

At the time of its release, it was available only to UK fans via two versions: an interactive version, running 13 minutes, on Oculus Store and Vive Port, or a 360-degree version, running 11 minutes, on BBC VR App. International fans have been promised a release of the game at a later date.

Doctor Who: Edge of Time

Released in November to PS4 and PC after a short delay is *Doctor Who: Edge of Time*, a brand-new virtual reality video game. It is based on the long-running BBC science fiction show and was developed by Maze Theory and published by PlayStack.

When I recently got to view some of the game play, it definitely gave me a bit of a *BioShock* feel as one gets to explore through time and space, stunning cinematic environments, along with the 13th Doctor's sonic screwdriver in hand, using it to assist the player in solving a variety of puzzles and unlocking doors.

In a press release from the BBC, Maze Theory creative director, Marcus Moresby stated, "Maze Theory is committed to re-defining storytelling through awesome, innovative and immersive experiences in virtual reality. *Doctor Who* is an incredibly exciting and timeless franchise with a passionate and committed global fan base. We are looking to give them an entirely new experience; an opportunity to team-up with The Doctor and feel like they are in the show. This of course includes piloting the TARDIS, a dream come true for fans!"

The game features many of *Doctor Who* favorite villains including the Daleks and the Weeping Angels as well as stars the voice talent of the 13th Doctor, Jodie Whittaker.

Being a huge fan of video games myself, this is one game I'm really looking forward to getting my hands on to play. Look for it on PlayStation VR, Oculus Rift, Oculus Quest, HTC VIVE and VIVE Cosmos.

Appendix E: Doctor Who Magazine

Doctor Who Magazine

Doctor Who Magazine (DWM) is a monthly magazine, initially published by Marvel Comics in 1979. Now, published by Panini Comics, the magazine is about all things *Doctor Who*, featuring news, reviews, interviews, comic strips, etc. It is currently recognized by the Guinness World Records as the world's longest-running TV tie-in magazine.

Jodie Whittaker and her Doctor has appeared on the cover of the magazine at least seven times since her announcement in 2018. Issues of the magazine can be purchased individually or through a digital or print subscription online.

https://www.amazon.com/Doctor-Who-Magazine/dp/B01MT21ZIS

Appendix F: Doctor Who Conventions

Doctor Who Conventions

While over the recent years, many *Doctor Who* conventions have struggled to survive state-wide, there are some fantastic ones still going strong around the world:

Chicago TARDIS
Con Kasterborous
Gallifrey One
L.I. Who
SD Who Con
TimeLash (Germany)
Vworp (UK)
Whooverville (UK)

Appendix G: Doctor Who Immersive Adventures

Doctor Who Time Fracture: An Immersive Adventure

Coming to central London in Autumn 2020 is *Doctor Who Time Fracture: An Immersive Adventure*, a theatrical event unlike anything before that puts the audience into the heart of the story of *Doctor Who*.

A gateway has opened underneath the streets of London, causing a rip in time and space as we currently know it, which has started to collapse. Now, it is YOUR turn to be the hero and save planet Earth, as you travel across the universe meeting new creatures, facing new challenges and exploring new worlds.

A Gallifreyan Coin token can be purchased through the *Doctor Who Time Fracture: An Immersive Adventure* website and will be permitted to be redeemed at a later date for a ticket to a performance.

If you liked this show, you might like

Torchwood
Firefly
The Sarah Janes Adventures
Class
Years and Years
Star Trek

Acknowledgments

A special thank you to those who took time out of their days to be interviewed for this book, including Beth Axford, Will Brooks, Christian Basel, Krystal Moore, Alisa Stern, Ken Deep, Wendy Abrahams, and Stephen Hatcher.

To David Valentin for assisting in ads and social media. I'm looking forward to reading your book when it comes out!

To Riverdale Avenue Books for approaching me with such a fantastic idea and line of books.

To Jodie Whittaker and Chris Chibnall—this book wouldn't be possible without you both

End Notes

Team, T. D. W. (2017, July 16). Doctor Who—Introducing Jodie Whittaker—The Thirteenth Doctor. Retrieved from http://www.bbc.co.uk/blogs/doctor who/entries/399b321f-63cb-4b83-8bd3-e6874d09579f

Who, D. (2017, July 16). Thirteenth Doctor Reaction | Doctor Who: The Fan Show. Retrieved from http://www.youtube.com/watch?v=LWLrgmOECbw

Dwtv. (2017, July 18). BBC Reports "Overwhelmingly Positive" Response to 13 Reveal. Retrieved from http://www.doctorwhotv.co.uk/bbc-reports-overwhelm ingly-positive-response-to-13-reveal-85918.htm

Association, P. (2018, October 8). Jodie Whittaker's Doctor Who a ratings hit with highest launch in 10 years. Retrieved from http://www.telegraph.co.uk/ tv/2018/10/08/jodie-whittakers-doctor-ratings-hit-highest-launch-10-years/

Kistler, A. (2013). *Doctor Who: A History*. Guilford, Connecticut: Lyons Press, An imprint of Globe Pequot Press.

Foundation, S. A. G.-A. F. T. R. A. (2016, April 21). Conversations with David Tennant. Retrieved from http://www.youtube.com/watch?v=rjBswS_1nq0

Knapp, A. (2013, November 22). Why Doctor Who Has Lasted Fifty Years. Retrieved from https://www.forbes. com/sites/alexknapp/2013/11/22/why-doctor-who-has-lasted-fifty-years/#6cc746995900

Rice, B. (2015, June 15). Doctor Who Creator Sydney Newman Wanted a Female Doctor. Retrieved from https://doctorwhowatch.com/2015/06/15/doctor-who-creator-sydney-newman-wanted-a-female-doctor/

Seddon, Dan. "Former BBC Boss Defends Doctor Who's Original Axe." *Digital Spy*, Digital Spy, 3 Oct. 2019, https://www.digitalspy.com/tv/a29349197/doctor-who-news-science-fiction-garbage/?fbclid=IwAR120VFIgs gPSbydfyFFDkz1c_-R5QdzuKPJygkskjfyayEKcifIoL 8wARk

Foundation, S. A. G.-A. F. T. R. A. (2016, April 21). Conversations with David Tennant. Retrieved from http://www.youtube.com/watch?v=rjBswS_1nq0

Hastings, C. (2019, September 15). Doctor Who star Christopher Eccleston reveals his battle with anorexia almost drove him to suicide. Retrieved from http://www.dailymail.co.uk/tvshowbiz/article-7464325/Doctor -star-Christopher-Eccleston-reveals-battle-anorexia-drove-suicide.html?fbclid=IwAR2_KG9oLhkmWhCV vYAawRAr_WjsWJN9mpQxPHNltVBo-5nLVQPuL W7T66A

Christopher Eccleston says he "lost faith and trust and belief" in Doctor Who bosses while filming. (2018, March 20). Retrieved from http://www.radiotimes.com/news/tv/2018-03-19/doctor-who-christopher-eccleston-russell-t-davies/

Dietrich, D. (2019, September 15). Christopher Eccleston's Panel at Rose City Comic Con. Retrieved from https://www.youtube.com/watch?v=GvjPy6n5hKc

McEwan, C. K. (2018, November 29). The reasons why each Doctor Who actor quit. Retrieved from https://www.digitalspy.com/tv/a854678/doctor-who-actors-quit-david-tennant-matt-smith/

What would Doctor Who Series 5 have looked like if David Tennant had stayed on? (n.d.). Retrieved from http://www.doctorwho.tv/whats-new/article/what-would-doctor-who-series-5-have-looked-like-if-david-tennant-had-stayed-on

Jeffery, M. (2018, November 27). What Doctor Who 5 would look like with Tennant. Retrieved from https://www.digitalspy.com/tv/cult/a847706/doctor-who-series-5-david-tennant-steven-moffat-storyline/

Hastings, C. (2009, January 3). Matt Smith announced as new Doctor Who. Retrieved from https://www.telegraph.co.uk/culture/tvandradio/4092973/Matt-Smith-announced-as-new-Doctor-Who.html

French, D. (2018, November 7). Matt Smith rejected for BBC's 'Sherlock'. Retrieved from http://www.

digitalspy.com/tv/cult/a201372/matt-smith-rejected-for-bbcs-sherlock/

Fullerton, Huw. "Jodie Whittaker on Auditioning for Matt Smith's Doctor Who Series: 'Thank Goodness I Didn't Get It!'." *Radio Times*, 26 Sept. 2018, https://www.radiotimes.com/news/tv/2018-09-25/jodie-whittaker-on-auditioning-for-matt-smiths-doctor-who-series-thank-goodness-i-didnt-get-it/?fbclid=IwAR0v XHstE8MAcWqOkMZFafhN2suq4z8w90Dc1X5ddjV3 4z8ZvCsi8djS4UI

Matt Smith Is Leaving Doctor Who, It's Official. (n.d.). Retrieved from http://www.giantfreakinrobot.com/scifi/matt-smith-leaving-doctor-official. html

Peter Capaldi on leaving Doctor Who: "I want to always be giving it my best and I don't think if I stayed on I'd be able to do that". (2017, August 10). Retrieved from https://www.radiotimes.com/news/2017-06-19/peter-capaldi-on-leaving-doctor-who-i-want-to-always-be-giving-it-my-best-and-i-dont-think-if-i-stayed-on-id-be-able-to-do-that/

Grierson, Jamie. "Doctor Who Casting: Time Lords Clash over 'Loss of Role Model for Boys'." *The Guardian*, Guardian News and Media, 21 July 2017, www.theguardian.com/tv-and-radio/2017/jul/21/doctor-who-casting-peter-davison-laments-loss-of-role-model-for-boys

America, B. B. C. (2018, October 7). New York Comic-Con 2018 | Full Doctor Who Panel | New Episodes

Premiere Sundays at 8 p.m. Retrieved from https://www.youtube.com/watch?v=2VnEdqRpjnc

Young, S. (2018, October 11). If You Thought You'd Never Be a Whovian, Jodie Whittaker Might Just Change Your Mind. Retrieved from https://www.bustle.com/p/jodie-whittaker-wants-her-doctor-who-to-be-accessible-to-everyone-including-you-12211213

Hearn, M. (2018, October). Rosa. *Doctor Who Magazine*, (531), 18—19

Manente, K. (2018, October 9). NYCC 2018: A New Era of 'Doctor Who' Embraces Inclusivity. Retrieved from https://www.geek.com/television/nycc-2018-a-new-era-of-doctor-who-embraces-inclusivity-1755088/

Who, D. (2018, July 23). FULL Comic-Con Panel | Doctor Who. Retrieved from http://www.youtube.com/watch?v=GGpi2Jmbr4M

Cook, Emily. "Top of the Bill." *Doctor Who Magazine*, 2018, pp. 14—16

Cook, Emily. "The Chase Is On." *Doctor Who Magazine*, Dec. 2018, p. 14.

Kerblam! (2019, August 26). Retrieved from https://en.wikipedia.org/wiki/Kerblam!

Kirkley, Paul. "'Doctor Who': Jodie Whittaker Won't Watch Classic Episodes until She Quits the Role (Exclusive)." *Yahoo!*, Yahoo!, 25 Sept. 2018, https://www.yahoo.com/entertainment/doctor-jodie-whittaker-wont-watch-classic-episodes-quits-role-exclusive-094848845.html

Fullerton, Huw. "The New Doctor Who Theme Tune Includes Recordings of the 1963 Original." *Radio Times*, https://www.radiotimes.com/news/tv/2018-10-19/the-new-doctor-who-theme-tune-includes-recordings-of-the-1963-original/

"Partition of India." *Wikipedia*, Wikimedia Foundation, https://en.wikipedia.org/wiki/Partition_of_India

Guerrier, Simon. "Now We Are Witnesses." *Doctor Who Magazine*, Jan. 2019, p. 37

Cook, Emily. "Cabin Fever." *Doctor Who Magazine*, Jan. 2019, pp. 65—66

Bone, Christian. "Doctor Who Showrunner Says The Doctor's New Scarf Was Found By Accident." *We Got This Covered*, 14 Dec. 2018, https://wegotthiscovered.com/tv/doctor-showrunner-reveals-doctors-scarf-accident

Laford, Andrea. "Doctor Who Series 12: Jodie Whittaker Reports on Filming Progress from Cardiff." *CultBox*, 4 Oct. 2019, https://cultbox.co.uk/news/doctor-who-series-12-jodie-whittaker-reports-on-filming-progress-from-cardiff?fbclid=IwAR1yOPRikYNQFmvGi-6UgSmehz2Br1GjcI-72n_7CfqDB-XkCmA8z7J4H3g

Fullerton, Huw. "Jodie Whittaker to Face the Judoon in New Doctor Who Series." Radio Times, May 22, 2019. https://www.radiotimes.com/news/tv/2019-05-21/jodie-whittaker-to-face-the-judoon-in-new-doctor-who-series/

Fullerton, Huw. "Doctor Who Boss Teases Classic Monsters Returning and a New Storyline for Yaz in 2020 Series." Radio Times. Accessed October 3, 2019. https://www.radiotimes.com/news/tv/2019-04-23/doctor-who-boss-teases-classic-monsters-returning-and-a-new-storyline-for-yaz-in-2020-series/

Houser, Jody. "Doctor Who: The Thirteenth Doctor X-Mas Special #1." Titan Comics. Accessed October 3, 2019. https://titan-comics.com/c/1511-doctor-who-the-thirteenth-doctor-x-mas-special/

Wegotthiscovered. "Jodie Whittaker And Chris Chibnall Rumored To Leave Doctor Who In 2019." We Got This Covered, November 21, 2018. https://wegotthiscovered.com /tv/jodie-whittaker-chris-chibnall-rumored-leave-doctor-2019/

"The Runaway (Video Game)." Tardis, May 2019. https://tardis.fandom.com/wiki/The_Runaway_(video_g ame)

New, Daniel. "Doctor Who: The Edge Of Time Is a New VR Game for PS4 and PC." Thumbsticks, May 20, 2019. https://www.thumbsticks.com/doctor-who-edge-of-time-oculus-psvr-05202019/

About the Author

Mackenzie grew up in the heartland of America, chasing leprechauns and rainbows, and dreaming of angels. Her parents nurtured a love of fantasy and make-believe by introducing her, from a young age, to the artistic and cultural opportunities that the city of Cleveland had to offer

She is a multi-award-winning novelist and in-demand speaker for conferences and conventions including **Rochester Writers' Conference, Wizard World, Imaginarium** (*Why Audio? Why Now—A Big Finish Productions Discussion with Chris Walker-Thomson*), **ConFusion** (*The 13th Doctor*), **MarCon** (*Controversial Topics in Sci-Fi Fandoms*), **Gallifrey One** (*How The Doctor Helps Us Better Understand Who We Are, Accept Ourselves, And Begin To Find Hope As We Heal*), etc., actively discussing the process of writing and *Doctor Who*. She is also an active panelist on *The Legend of the Traveling Tardis Radio Show* and has done book signings previously at Who North America, the largest *Doctor Who* store, and museum located in the United States in the state of Indiana.

Her publishing portfolio includes the following books: *The Rite of Wands* (BHC Press, 2017), *The Whispered Tales of Graves Grove* (BHC Press, 2017),

Unknown Realms (Fiction-Atlas Press, 2019), *The Binge Watcher's Guide to Doctor Who: Season 11, Jodie Whittaker,* (Riverdale Avenue Books, 2019) and *The Rite of Abnegation* (BHC Press, 2020).

A storyteller at heart, she loves to inspire the imagination. Mackenzie makes her home in Mount Morris, Michigan, where she is currently penning her next adventure.

If you liked this book,
Please join our mailing list at riverdaleavebooks.com
We will be publishing 13 volumes of
The Binge Watcher's Guide to Doctor Who

You Might Also Enjoy These other Riverdale Avenue Books Pop Culture Titles

How to Throw a True Blood Party: An Unofficial Guide
By Paula Conway

Norman Reedus: True Tales of the Walking Dead's Zombie Hunter
By Marc Shapiro

Welcome to Shondaland: An Unauthorized Biography of Shonda Rhimes
By Marc Shapiro

You're Gonna Make It After All: The Life and Times and Influence of Mary Tyler Moore
By Marc Shapiro